I0520109

POWERFUL

BY
M.G. COLL

First Published in 2018 by Blossom Spring Publishing
Powerful Copyright © 2018 M.G. Coll
ISBN 978-1-9996490-4-3
E: admin@blossomspringpublishing.com
W: www.blossomspringpublishing.com
Published in the United Kingdom. All rights reserved under
International Copyright Law. Contents and/or cover may
not be reproduced in whole or in part without the express
written consent of the publisher.
This is a work of fiction. Names, characters, places and
incidents are either products of the author's imagination or
are used fictitiously. Any resemblance to actual events or
locales or persons, living or dead, save those clearly in the
public domain, is purely coincidental.

No matter how many times you get knocked down, never give up on your dreams. If you do, you will miss out on the most amazing experiences life has to offer!

M.G. Coll

CHAPTER ONE

Click, clack. Click, clack. With each step she took, her stiletto heels reverberated loudly against the white marble floor. Her heart beat a thousand miles per minute. The white hallways all looked the same, but she knew where she was going. She had been down this same path far too many times. But, tonight was different. She was not following orders, she was acting on her own.

Before turning the corner, she stopped and took a deep breath. This was important – too important to mess up. All was riding on this. There were no second chances.

"It's going to be okay," she whispered to herself.

After some seconds had passed, she finally found the courage to keep walking. As she came closer to the high security area, time seemed to stop. The guard on night watch looked up at the sound of her approaching steps.

"Dr. Harmon, what brings you here at this hour?" he asked, not hiding the suspicion in his tone.

She cleared her throat and tried to sound as calm and natural as possible, ignoring the panic in the back of her mind.

"I'm here on Snyde's orders," she said, staring him in the eye. "He wants to run some last minute tests on the children. Can't wait until tomorrow, unfortunately. He thinks he is onto something big. But, that's highly classified, as you well know."

"Oh – yes, of course," said the guard, his tone had a nervous edge. "Step right on through."

She nodded and proceeded. First, she placed her palm on the initial hand scan. A blood scan, retinal scan and facial recognition came next.

This had better work. You had better be waiting at the rendezvous point, Finn, or I will kill you, she thought. Taking another deep breath, she stepped forward. The room she had entered was plain, no decorations, no colour, only four plain cots, two on each side.

"Sammy, Mikey, get up. Quickly!" she said, her tone serious.

"Alex?" asked Samantha, stifling a yawn. "What's wrong?"

"Nothing, we're just going on a small field trip," said Alexa. "Come on, hurry up! We don't have much time. Mikey, take Amelia, I'll get Polo. Go, quickly! As quietly as possible."

****

Heavy rain poured down on Finn Cready's face. Each drop felt like cold needles piercing his skin, yet he knew he had to keep running. He could not stop. If he just kept going he would finally escape, he would be safe. *They* would be safe.

When Finn had made a plan to escape the facility where he had been working for almost ten years, he knew it would be dangerous. He had not however, thought it could have so many flaws. He had triggered an alarm and was now being chased down. Hunted.

He could hear guards closing in and kept running. The rendezvous point had to be close. Alexa would be waiting with the children.

"Come on, Finn" he said to himself. "Just a bit longer, you can do this. You've made it this far."

At this precise moment he heard it. A howl that made his hairs stand on end. They couldn't have possibly sent *them* after him. They weren't supposed to be ready for the field. He heard another terrible howl. They were getting closer.

A deep fear grew inside Finn. He knew why these creatures had been designed. They were wild, savage dogs. Bred and created to kill, to destroy. Chemically enhanced to do as much damage as humanly possible. They were part of the newest phase of the project. War Dogs, as Doctor Oleander Snyde had very lovingly baptised them.

The howling and barking got louder as they came closer. There was a high chance they had already picked up his scent. God help him. He needed to get out of here.

He began to run again, as fast as his legs could take him. Ten steps, twenty, thirty. Then he felt his feet stumble. As he shook his head to recover his surroundings, he heard a rustling behind him. He dared turn. His eyes fell on what he had been fearing. Monstrous creatures, almost as big as bears, yellow fangs bared, drool dripping from their open mouths. War dogs. These creatures were far from normal. Their fur had the texture of burnt charcoal and their bodies released intense amounts of heat.

One of the dogs launched itself towards Finn, knocking the air from him, pinning him to the ground. The dog bared its teeth and growled. Slowly, it seemed to catch on fire. Its body contorted in an unnatural way, its charcoal fur cracking, sprouting small flames that flickered in the darkness, lighting the black night.

Just as he prepared for the pain that would come from the first bite, Finn heard a loud crashing noise forcing his eyes open again. A truck sped straight towards him. It hit the two other dogs and knocked them unconscious. The first dog took its attention away from Finn and went for the truck. It opened its jaw wide and began to inhale the sharp air around it. Finn could feel it, like a whirlwind around him.

The air rushed past his jacket, leaves and branches flew wildly towards the creature. From its gaping mouth, it released a jet of flaming orange fire. It hit the left side of the truck with full force, causing it to stop.

"Finn!" Alex called from inside the truck. "Maybe you could hurry up? We're in a bit of a mess, in case you haven't noticed!"

With all the strength he could manage he stood up and ran towards the truck, opened the driver side door and pushed Alex out of the way.

"How nice of you to join us!" Alex huffed. "Now, come on, Finn, we have to get out of here. This truck can't take much more of this.

"Finn!" Samantha called out from the back seat. "Are you hurt?" Concern in her small voice.

"I'm okay, Sammy," he said and managed a weak smile. "Just some minor burns, nothing too serious."

"It's probably worse than you think!" squeaked Michael, sitting beside Samantha.

Michael was six years old, tall for his age. His big brown eyes glowed with excitement, as if they were on a fun adventure. Next to him sat two other kids. Amelia, only two years old, and Apollo, who had just turned three a few weeks ago.

The four kids had been born at the facility, never knowing anything about life outside this place – this prison.

"Shut up, Mikey," said Samantha. "This isn't a game, you know?" Samantha was the eldest of the four kids. She was seven years old and very mature for her age. She constantly disagreed with almost every word Michael spoke.

Finn wondered how much they actually understood about their present situation. They were just kids, after all. He only hoped they would all get through this, so he could explain everything when they were old enough.

"We've got to keep moving," said Alexa.

He nodded and stepped on the gas.

"We're almost at the fence," said Alexa. "Once we get past that, we'll be safe."

"Let's hope there are no more set backs," said Finn.

"What happened, Finn?" she asked. "I thought they weren't supposed to notice we were gone until much later. We should have been able to get away without issues."

"I... I made a mistake," said Finn. "I had to go back for something. Something important!" He added harshly, as soon as he saw the furious expression on Alexa's face.

"You put us all in danger because you decided to go back for something?" she yelled. "What was so important?"

Finn didn't answer.

"We must be getting close to the perimeter fence," he said, changing the subject.

He brought the truck to a stop in front of a thirty foot high perimeter fence. Their escape route. Once they cleared it, they should be home free. The fence, however, was electrified with no way around or above it. The voltage was so high that any contact with it would have left them with no escape vehicle, and probably cost them their lives in the process.

Alexa turned to the back seat where the kids sat, excited with their adventure.

"Okay, Sammy," she whispered, her gaze transfixed on the small girl's sparkling blue eyes. "It's all up to you now. Work your magic."

The little girl nodded. She closed her eyes in heavy concentration and took a deep breath. After a few seconds, the high fence started emitting a low humming noise, blue sparks of electricity shot out from all sides. Spark after spark lit up the rainy night sky. Blue sparks became tiny lights that seemed to leave the fence and dissolve into Samantha.

She absorbed the electricity that powered the fence. The fence continued to emit a few more sparks and all of a sudden, they stopped. Even though Finn knew she could do it, it still shocked him to see it happen. These four kids were no ordinary kids. They each possessed one very special ability. Samantha's was to generate, control and absorb all electric power.

Samantha leaned back in the seat, clearly exhausted from the effort of absorbing such a high electric charge.

"Are you alright, Sammy?" asked Finn, concern in his voice.

She nodded and gave him a weak smile. He hated putting her through this, and if they would have had any other choice he would have taken it, but this was the only way out.

"Okay, everyone hold on tight!" exclaimed Finn, he put his foot down on the gas pedal and the truck sped forward, crashing through the perimeter fence.

CHAPTER TWO

FIFTEEN YEARS LATER

"Are you sure about this, Polo?" asked Samantha, as she drove the old blue truck steadily down a dirt road in the middle of nowhere.

"I'm pretty sure," he answered. "Well, at least ninety nine percent sure." He gave her a wide grin.

She rolled her eyes at him but couldn't help but smile back. They had been driving for over an hour and still saw no signs of what they were looking for. Samantha gazed sideways at Apollo. His face was alight with expectation – mixed with a bit of fear. She knew him too well. He had never been a big risk taker, that sort of thing was more down her alley, yet he always insisted on being by her side through all of it.

This night, they had seen a news broadcast that had set them on a very particular search, one that had been ongoing for many years. To think that tonight they could finally achieve their goal was a feeling too great to put into words. It would be a victory after so many failures.

They continued in silence for a further ten minutes. Apollo put a hand on her shoulder.

"There," he pointed to their right.

"Yes, I see it."

There was a vast corn field and all of it was engulfed in bright orange flames. There wasn't an inch that didn't seem to be burning.

"That's definitely no forest fire," Apollo pointed out, pushing his glasses higher up his nose.

Samantha nudged him gently, "look, straight ahead."

"A police barricade."

"Those don't look like normal police though, do they?"

"Snyde Corp?"

"Probably, which means we are definitely in the right place."

Samantha kept driving towards the police barricade and stopped at their signal. She rolled down her window.

"Good evening, officer."

"Evening. I'm afraid I can't let you go this way. As you can see, we've got a very dangerous situation on our hands," said the officer.

"Clearly," said Samantha, dryly, not looking into the fake officer's face.

Apollo cleared his throat loudly, drawing the attention towards himself. "Excuse me, sir, can you tell us what could have caused this?"

The officer looked Apollo up and down. "Probably just the heat."

"It's the middle of October," said Samantha. "Not much heat anymore."

The officer gave her a look of annoyance. "Must be some idiot tossing a lit cigarette or punk kids lighting the field," the man said, offering a forced smile. "Why don't you just turn back and find a safer route?"

"Excellent idea, *officer*," said Samantha. She tightened her grip on the steering wheel and a small spark shot out of her hand.

"Thanks so much for the help, officer," said Apollo, quickly, attempting to distract the officer from noticing.

She started the truck again, making a U-turn and heading in the opposite direction.

"Are you crazy?" he asked her nervously. "I'm stressed out enough as it is."

"Oh, just relax, will you? I could have taken him out with just a snap of my fingers." She looked over at him and smiled. "Don't worry so much… Okay, I'll pull the truck over and hide it behind those trees, then we can continue on foot."

"Sounds like a plan," he said, smiling back. She always knew how to calm him. "Did you see that fire? It's so strong. How are we going to search for her safely? It's crazy."

"Why would she start this fire in the first place?"

"I don't know, maybe she was attacked."

"That's not likely," said Samantha. "If they had attacked her they wouldn't be setting up that barricade. They would have taken her already. I think they're searching for her, just like we are."

"Then, we have to make sure we find her first."

Samantha found a safe spot to stop the truck out of sight.

"Alright, this is it," she said, looking directly into Apollo's eyes. "We have to find her. If Snyde has his men here it must mean she's still close. He wouldn't waste resources on this if she wasn't."

Apollo nodded in agreement. "Listen, we should split up and that way we'll cover more ground."

Samantha wasn't too convinced about this idea. "We should stick together… We're stronger together, you know that."

He considered her words for a moment then shook his head. "The search would be faster. Nothing bad is going to happen. We can take these guys. I can take care of myself, Sam."

"Don't argue, you're not going to win this one," she said. "We are sticking together."

"Fine," he agreed after a moment.

"Is there a plan? This place is too big to be able to find her easily," she asked him.

"Well, I don't know quite how to explain it, but I can feel the air. There are places where the fire is new, and it has been burning for less time. That's where we have to go. If there are new fires, it means she's still there."

"You can *feel* the fire in the air?" asked Samantha. "I don't think I'll ever understand your abilities. They're too confusing... But it's the best chance we have, so let's try that. Lead the way."

He nodded, adjusted his glasses once more and got down from the truck. Samantha exited the truck after him and walked to stand beside him.

"Remember, let's try and be as discreet as possible, Sam. We don't really want full out combat here."

"I can't make any promises," she gave him a big grin. "You know how I enjoy a good fight."

"Never mind... Okay, let's go. This way, follow me."

They began walking slowly towards the field. It was hard to see with the amount of smoke that was filling the cool night air. Flames covered almost every inch of the immense field.

"Where's Michael when you need him?" asked Apollo.

"Forget about that, let's just find the safest path."

"This way." Apollo took the lead, walking slowly. Avoiding the flames as best he could.

Every now and then they stopped or found their path blocked by fire that they could not cross and had to backtrack and find a new way around. After a few minutes they spotted three of Snyde's men walking ahead of them. Two of the men walked ahead of the third.

Samantha put a finger to her lips to make sure Apollo didn't make a sound. They both stopped walking and crouched down, looking for a bit of cover. The men continued to walk in silence. Samantha charged her hands with electricity, the energy created blue and white sparks that covered her arms. She began to walk towards the man trailing behind and when she reached him, she snuck up behind him and shocked him with a jolt of electricity. Just enough to knock him out for a few hours. He didn't make a sound. The other two men continued walking without noticing their missing team member.

She crept up behind the last two. This time, she created two orbs of electricity in each hand and released them into the backs of the remaining men. They both dropped without a sound.

She turned to signal Apollo to continue. "See, I can behave myself," she told him.

"Great, let's keep going, shall we?" he coughed. "This smoke inhalation can't be any good for us."

"Relax, you'll live through it."

They walked for another twenty minutes and Samantha lost her patience. This search was getting them nowhere. With every minute that went by, they risked her running away, or worse.

"Are you sure you're leading us to the right place?" she asked exasperatedly.

"I'm doing my best, we just need to be patient."

"You're right. Sorry, I'm just anxious. It's too quiet. We haven't seen any more of Snyde's men. What if they already found her and took her?"

"I don't think so, I can still feel fresh fires. This way," he pointed to their left.

They walked and walked but didn't encounter anything or anyone.

"This is useless! Maybe we should go back and try another path, Polo."

Apollo suddenly dropped to his knees and pulled Samantha down with him.

"What are you doing? Have you completely lost your mind?" she asked angrily. "What did you –"

Apollo covered her mouth. "Be quiet," he whispered. "Look, over there."

He pointed to their right. Through the intense orange flames, you could make out the outline of an old barn. Walking in formation towards the barn were at least fifteen of Snyde's men, all dressed in black military style suits and heavily armed. They cautiously surrounded the barn.

"That has to be where she's hiding," said Apollo. "Now what do we do?"

Samantha thought about it for a few seconds and then said, "I'm going in. You cover me. I'll take out those men and once it's clear we'll go in after her."

"I'm not letting you fight them alone! It's crazy!"

"How very *gallant* of you, but I can take them. Trust me, you just make sure you cover me at the right times and they'll be no problem."

"You'll get hurt, I –"

Now it was Samantha who covered his mouth. "Stop worrying, will you? I'll be fine." Before he could argue any further, she kissed his cheek and sprinted off towards the barn.

"Sam!" he called out after her. "Damn it," he mumbled to himself. He got closer to make sure he would be able to cover her. With his powers he would be able to create forcefields and barriers from the air, protecting her from any shots they fired.

Samantha hurried towards the men, not bothering to use any stealth or find any cover. The men were spreading around the barn. They were all armed with automatic shotguns, which they aimed straight ahead. They still hadn't noticed her approaching. When she was only a few feet away from them, she called out. "Hey, I seem to have taken a wrong turn back there, care to point me in the right direction?"

The men looked confused, they didn't know how to react. Then, they saw her hands charge up with electricity.

"She's one of them!" One of the men called out to the others.

All together they focused their attention on Samantha and a few began to fire their weapons. The shots didn't get anywhere near her. The bullets fired, made contact with an invisible barrier and fell to the ground. Samantha smiled and ran towards the men.

More shots were fired. Again, they fell to the ground before making contact with their intended target.

"Stop! Don't forget our orders! The boss needs them alive!" shouted one man who was just approaching the scene. He appeared to have more seniority than the others.

Samantha took advantage of the brief distraction and ran closer, releasing two electric bolts towards the men closest to her. They fell to the ground. Then she ran towards a third man and kicked him hard to the ground. She placed a hand on his chest and knocked him out.

More shots fired. The bullets again fell short of the target. Four men came running towards her. They surrounded her, one of them grabbing her from behind.

"Bad idea." She charged her whole body with electricity and the man collapsed. She took out the other men easily and focused on the remaining ones still standing a short distance away.

"Call for backup, get reinforcements," the senior-looking man said.

Samantha headed towards the last men as they continued to shoot, no longer bothering to take proper aim. They were firing blindly. Suddenly one of the bullets got past the invisible barrier and grazed Samantha's side. She stumbled, grabbing the wound in pain, but quickly regained her stance. She charged herself with more power and released it towards the remaining men. They all fell to the ground, except one. The man calling the shots before had escaped. She could see him running away, probably to bring reinforcements. They had to move quickly.

Apollo came running from his hiding spot.

"Sam! Are you okay? I'm sorry! You were getting too far from my line of sight; the shields aren't strong enough at a distance. I knew I should have come with you."

"Don't worry about it," she said. "It's just a scratch, it'll heal in a few minutes. We don't have much time. One of them has gone for backup, and I don't think he'll bring just a dozen men this time."

Apollo nodded. "We have to find her."

They ran towards the barn and stepped inside. The barn was in complete darkness. Samantha charged her hand to create some light around them. The place seemed to be deserted. There were some old, abandoned horse paddocks and old bails of hay, multiple cobwebs and heaps of dirt all around.

"You think she's still here?" asked Apollo.

"I really don't know," she answered.

"Amelia!" Apollo yelled out.

No answer. They both walked slowly around the barn calling out her name. Still no one answered.

"This is a waste of time, she's not here anymore," Samantha sighed, standing in the middle of the barn, next to Apollo.

As she said this, a giant burst of fire came hurtling towards them. Apollo pulled Samantha away from the flames just in time. They both fell to the ground, Apollo banging his head against the hard floor, Samantha landing on top of him.

"You were saying?" asked Apollo, massaging the newly formed bump on his head.

Samantha looked furious. She picked herself up and pulled him with her. "Amelia! Stop! We're here to help you!" Apollo called out.

"How do I know you're not with *them?*" Asked a voice from behind one of the horse paddocks.

"Oh, come on! Are you serious? Maybe due to the fact that we almost got ourselves killed trying to stop them finding you first!" Samantha yelled.

Slowly, Amelia stepped out from her hiding place. She looked terrified and lacking sleep. Her dark red hair was matted and dirty, her clothes ripped in places and she looked like she hadn't had a decent meal in a while.

"You can trust us," said Apollo, he walked towards her slowly.

"Stay back!" warned Amelia. "How do you know my name? Why should I trust you?"

A small burst of fire shot out from her hands, onto the floor right beside her.

"Listen, we're here to help you. We know your name because we know you, from long ago, you were just too young to remember. I'm Apollo and this is Samantha."

****

15

Amelia studied them. These names did sound familiar, from some long forgotten past that was too jumbled to remember clearly. She didn't know what to think. Here were these two people, just asking her to trust them when she knew nothing about them.

First, they both looked like models, way too attractive in their own ways. They looked out of place in this dirty old barn. The girl, Samantha, looked surly and serious, with her dark blonde hair tied back into a long ponytail, an expression of deep annoyance on her face. Apollo on the other hand seemed somewhat cheerful. He was tall and thin, his brown eyes were soft and filled with kindness, his black hair was cut short but messy, the thick rimmed glasses resting on his nose and white buttoned down shirt with a small bowtie around the neck gave him a similar look to Clark Kent.

"We haven't got time for this," said Samantha. "If you want to be safe you have to come with us, otherwise, you can stay here and take your chances with them! Either way, I'm leaving now."

She turned and walked towards the barn's entrance.

"Sam!" Apollo called after here, she didn't pay attention to him and left the barn.

"Please, Amelia, just come with us. We'll have time to explain everything later, I promise. You have no idea how long we've been searching for you. We're just like you. These guys would love a chance to catch all of us, let's not give them that pleasure." He held out his hand towards her. Her green eyes were scanning him. An intense battle was taking place inside her mind. Was this a trap? Could she really trust them?

Nothing made sense to her. She looked from his hand to his face. His expression was kind, his hazel eyes sincere. She had put her trust in the wrong people before, it had never worked out well for her. People had always let her down, one way or another. Taking a deep breath, she reluctantly stretched her own hand and took his.

They ran out of the barn together. Outside stood Samantha, waiting for them. Her look of annoyance had not changed. In fact, it seemed to have intensified.

"I thought you would be back at the truck by now," said Apollo.

"I probably should be," answered Samantha, rather bluntly. "Can we go now?"

The other two nodded. All the fields were still burning, flames surrounded almost everything by now.

"Can't you do something about these fires? Make them disappear so we can get back to the truck easily."

Amelia blushed and felt a bit ashamed. "No, I – I don't really know how to control it. The fires just start on their own, I can never make them go away."

"You mean you didn't cause this fire on purpose?" asked Apollo.

Amelia shook her head. "I – I was looking for a place to spend the night. The fire just started, it began to spread everywhere. Once it started I couldn't stop it. Then, those men came… and I ran… The fire continued to spread."

"Never mind, let's just get going," said Samantha.

She had barely finished her sentence when shots were fired in their direction. Amelia screamed, Apollo created a shield around them.

"Great, they're back," said Samantha, angrily. "The two of you, start running towards the truck. I'll hold them off and catch up to you."

"Sam, no, let's stick together," said Apollo.

"Don't worry, I'll be right behind you. Just go, run. As fast as you can."

Apollo nodded, still a bit reluctant. He turned to Amelia, "keep hold of my hand and run as fast as you can. Don't look back, we'll be okay."

She gave him a nervous nod and then the two of them began to run. They could hear shots being fired behind them but didn't turn around. They ran as fast as they could, slowing down only to avoid the fires they encountered along the way.

After running for fifteen minutes they saw the truck at a distance. "Come one, we're almost there," Apollo tried to encourage her. They reached the truck panting. Apollo looked back anxiously, searching for any trace that Samantha was behind them. She was nowhere in sight.

"Where is she?" he asked. "She said she'd be right behind us." He began pacing nervously around the truck. "Maybe I should go back and help her."

"No! You can't leave me here alone!" Amelia exclaimed. She was on the verge of tears. "She looks like she can take care of herself."

"She can, but sometimes she's a bit hot headed and tries to take on too much, she may be injured or need some help."

"There she is!" Amelia pointed to the field, where Samantha was running towards them, clutching her left arm.

Apollo heaved a great sigh of relief.

"Hurry! Get in the truck!" Samantha yelled at them.

"What's wrong?" Apollo called back.

"Just – get – in – the – truck!" she yelled again, she was gasping for air with each word.

They both did as they were told. Samantha reached the truck and got in the driver's seat. She started the engine and accelerated like crazy.

"Are they following us?" asked Amelia. She caught a glimpse of Samantha's left arm. It was gushing blood. "What happened to you?"

"I'm alright, it's nothing."

"It doesn't *look* like nothing. Is that a *bite?*" Apollo asked.

Samantha nodded. "I don't know what they were… They were these huge animals – like wolves or wild dogs – but the size of bears. My powers didn't seem to do them much harm. They absorbed the energy I threw at them."

"That's not good," said Amelia, she sat in the back seat, shaking from head to toe. This day was not going at all how she had planned. All she had wanted was a safe place to stay the night, before continuing on her way.

"No, it's not. I only just got away, but they were still following me."

She sped the truck as fast as she could. Suddenly there was a loud bang in the back of the truck. The truck swerved a bit on the road. Amelia screamed. Right behind them were two of the giant enhanced dogs, growling and howling, their teeth bared.

"Polo, use your powers to try and push them back," said Samantha, as she tried to keep them from ramming the truck again.

Apollo turned to look at the dogs and sent a strong burst of wind towards one of them. The dog tripped and fell, but in a few seconds was back on his feet.

"Umm…it doesn't seem to be very effective!" he said.

The other dog rammed hard against the side of the truck, almost causing it to turn on its side. "We have to do something," said Samantha.

19

Amelia glanced at Samantha's face. The stoic expression was replaced by worry. Fear began to creep in. If these dogs could worry Samantha, then they must be a real threat.

"Try again, Polo, a stronger attack this time."

Once again, Apollo focused on one of the dogs. This time, he created a much stronger gust of wind and sent it directly at the dog. It stumbled again, falling a bit behind. He focused on the other dog and did the same. Both dogs were now further away from the truck, but they were quickly trying to catch up.

"Amelia, try using your fire on them, maybe it will slow them down."

"No! No way, I told you I can't control it! I could blow us up accidentally or something! I always hurt someone without meaning to."

"Well, that's the point! We need to hurt those dogs, or they'll definitely hurt us!" Samantha said. "Just give it a try, will you?"

"I can't!"

"There is a high chance we are going to die!" shouted Samantha. "Just try and help!"

Amelia's terror was written on her face. She was afraid of her powers, hated them even. But now she had to try and help. She focused on one of the dogs. Nothing was happening. "I can't!"

The dogs were closing in. "Forget it!" yelled Samantha.

One of the dogs reached the side of the truck again. Samantha launched the truck towards it, hitting the dog as hard as possible. It fell to the ground with a yelp. The second dog came closer. Apollo shot out another gust of wind, knocking it on its side. Amelia was screaming at the top of her lungs.

"I think they're getting tired!" shouted Apollo. "They're falling behind. Just floor it! Let's get out of here!"

Samantha had her foot down as far as the pedal would go. The dogs had in fact stopped chasing them. She watched them grow smaller and smaller in the rearview mirror and eventually disappear from sight.

"Are you both okay?" asked Samantha.

"Yes, we're fine," said Apollo.

Amelia nodded. She wanted to speak, her mind struggled to find words and mouth could not form them. She felt like she might collapse. Then, as if on cue, she fainted.

CHAPTER THREE

"Is she still out cold?" Samantha asked.

She drove the old truck down a deserted dirt road. They were approaching their destination.

"Yep, still out like a log," said Apollo.

He sat in the back seat, Amelia lay with her head on his lap. She had not regained consciousness from their encounter with the War Dogs. Samantha met his gaze in the rearview mirror.

"She hasn't died on us, has she?" Samantha asked. "After all the trouble we've gone through to find her, it would be incredibly ironic."

"Nope, she is still very much alive," said Apollo.

"Well, we'll be home soon," she said. "If she's not awake by then we'll just have to carry her."

She took a left turn into an unmarked road, very easy to miss for people unfamiliar with the area. It was unpaved, steep and narrow, the trail leading to the mountains. Not many people would dare wander through here, day or night. Multiple tight curves, thick bushes and trees made this piece of land almost impossible to drive. Not for Samantha. She knew them like the back of her hand.

After a few minutes they reached what appeared to be a dead end. The mountain blocked the way and no more road was visible. The only thing for miles was a waterfall. Heavy curtains of water poured down from the top. To the naked eye, this was the end of the road. What any lost wanderer would not notice was that behind this waterfall was a small cave with a secret chamber leading to an underground tunnel. The perfect camouflage.

Samantha drove the truck without any hesitation, as she had done on countless occasions, through the waterfall and stopped in the middle of the dark cave. She put the vehicle in neutral as a blue light beam scanned the truck. Once the blue beam had finished its inspection, the ground beneath them began to rumble. The truck was slowly lowered, deeper and deeper into the cave.

They came to a stop at an underground parking garage. Two more trucks were parked nearby, one of them no longer operational. Samantha halted the truck near the main entrance and hopped out.

"Come on, Polo," said Samantha. "Let's take her inside. She needs to get cleaned up and to get some real rest."

"Sure," said Apollo. "How about I carry her, you take care of the grooming. Deal?"

"Sounds like a plan," said Samantha, smiling.

With a nod, he picked Amelia up and carried her inside.

****

Amelia opened her eyes and sat up quickly. She was disoriented, her pulse beating madly. Her heart pounding against her chest. She had the most terrible headache. Blinking, her eyes darted across the room, everything was unfamiliar and strange. Where was she? How did she get here? Everything about the previous night was a blur. The last thing she remembered were the dogs retreating. After that, everything had turned to darkness.

It took her a couple of minutes to process that she did, in fact, appear to be at a safe place. She glanced around the room, trying to understand where this place was. There was a large 65" TV set, a dark wooden desk with a small laptop resting on top, a walk-in closet and a bathroom. She tried to get up from the bed but felt a bit weak and sat back down. When was the last time she had a proper meal? Maybe last week. She wasn't sure. She ran her hands through her hair. It felt incredibly silky and clean. Had they given her a shower?

She was wearing fresh clothes as well. Clean sweat pants and T-shirt. The bed she sat on was huge, king size. The mattress felt glorious, it was soft and well cushioned. This was a far stretch from the last bed she remembered sleeping on. The sheets were dark blue and smelled of fresh lavender. Everything was so luxurious. The exact opposite of what she was accustomed to.

She stood from her bed and came to admire the room's floor. It was shiny white marble. She could almost make out her reflection on it. Walking towards the closet, she felt even more amazed. It was the size of a small room. There was too much space, compared to the amount of clothes that filled it. There were a few pairs of jeans, variety of shirts and shoes. She picked up a pair and examined it carefully.

Was she dreaming? She must be. There was no other explanation for this. It did not make any sense that she would suddenly wake up in a room that was almost too perfect. With everything she could possibly need. She nodded her head and decided, she was most definitely dreaming. She would allow it to play out for a while, after all, this was much better than anything from her reality.

While standing in the middle of the gigantic closet, her stomach growled loudly. When was the last time she ate? Walking towards the bathroom she was able to fully glance at herself in the mirror. Her face was gaunt, her skin felt dry and sallow. She looked even worse than she felt, in her opinion. At least she looked cleaner than she had in the last year.

After a few minutes staring at her reflection she decided it was time to find some food. She shyly stepped out of the room and into the hall. It was a wide hallway with dark grey walls and the same shiny marble floors as the previous room. There were three doors next to the one she had just come from. She began walking slowly down the hall, not sure if it was okay to go wherever she pleased. Then again, if this was her dream, she could pretty much do as she wished.

When she reached the end of the hall she heard voices. She stopped and tried to listen to what was being said.

"Look, I know what you mean, but she's one of us, we have to try and help her," Amelia recognized Apollo's voice.

"You saw her powers, she can't control them," said Samantha. "She's dangerous, to herself and others. There is no telling what she could do. Her powers are too strong. Not being able to control them could cause real mayhem."

"But, don't you remember how I was? And you helped me learn to control my abilities," he argued.

"I'm not saying I won't help her, I'm just saying that she needs a *lot* of help and maybe I'm not the right person for it."

"Please, Sam, do it for me," said Apollo. "We're all she's got."

"I know that, I'm not trying to be a bitch about this, really," said Samantha. "It's not like I'm going to kick her out on the street. You know I'll try to train her. I'm just worried. If she doesn't learn how to control her powers, we will all be in danger."

"Don't be dramatic," said Apollo. "Nothing bad is going to happen. This is the first really good thing to happen to us in a long time. You know how long it's taken, so much searching. She is finally back home, where she belongs."

"I know… I'm sorry, I don't mean to complain… It's just…"

"What?" he asked.

"It's just not what I was expecting, I guess," she said, her tone slightly defeated. "Go and check on her, will you? She's been out for a whole day already."

"She must be exhausted," he said. "I'll go and check."

Okay, it was settled. Not a dream. Amelia held her breath and before he could turn into the hall and realize that she had been eavesdropping on their conversation, stepped into the room. They were in a large living room, with a large black leather couch in which Samantha was sitting, legs stretched out, holding a book, Apollo sat across from her on a vast wooden table.

"Hey, we were just talking about you!" said Apollo, cheerfully. "I was just going to check up on you. How are you feeling?"

"Confused… Tired," replied Amelia. "And very hungry, to be honest."

"Come on, I'll fix you something to eat," said Samantha. She got up from the couch and walked into another room. Amelia stared at Apollo, who gave her a confident nod. She followed Samantha into what turned out to be a very modern looking kitchen. The cabinets were made of dark wood, there were two ovens mounted on the wall, an electric stovetop, black marble kitchen tops, a wide bench for food preparation, and a bench with five high metal stools around it. She took a seat, as Samantha picked a few things from the fridge and began to put together some sandwiches.

For some reason, Amelia found herself very intimidated by Samantha. There was something about her, she seemed so serious and formidable, not to mention the fact that she was very beautiful. Her long blonde hair came down in waves over her shoulders, her blue eyes had a certain sparkle to them. Without realizing it, she had been staring.

"Is something wrong?" asked Samantha.

"No, sorry… I um, didn't mean to stare," Amelia said nervously. "I'm a bit awkward around people sometimes. I've spent most of my time alone."

"Oh… Right... I really can't imagine what it's been like for you," said Samantha. "At least I had Alex, Mike and Polo. Finn took you and we never heard from either of you again."

Amelia nodded. For some reason, she remembered Finn, but couldn't remember anyone else. Maybe she didn't really remember Finn, and only thought this because he had been the only idea of a family for such a long time. He had always tried to protect her. Every now and then her dreams brought flashbacks of that night, up on the roof. She remembered a loud bang and then nothing. No one coming for her, there was just loneliness.

She had spaced off and only snapped back to reality when Samantha put down a plate with two large sandwiches in front of her.

"Thanks," said Amelia as she began to eat. She felt herself half eat and half devour the sandwich without even chewing. It tasted amazing, better than anything else she remembered eating in a very long time.

"I'll let you finish your food in peace," said Samantha. "But there are a few things we need to talk about after, okay?"

Amelia nodded. "Thank you... For everything. I know you risked your lives for me."

"Don't mention it," answered Samantha and she left the kitchen.

Amelia finished eating and cleaned up. She felt so much better now, like new life had been breathed into her. She walked out of the kitchen and back into the living room, where Apollo was sitting.

"Hey, how was your meal?" he asked, adjusting his glasses as she sat down next to him.

"It was great," she said. "Thank you so much for all you've done."

"Don't worry about it, it really isn't that big a deal," he said. "We have been been looking for you for such a long time now, we're just glad we finally found you and that you're safe and sound with us."

"Thanks – for trying to make me feel welcome."

"This is your home now," he said. "We want you to feel safe here. You should have been here with us from the very beginning... It's unfair that you didn't get that chance."

She nodded gratefully. Hearing the word *home* was something new and almost surreal for her. There was a hint of fear that if she got too comfortable it would all go away or maybe she would realize that this really had been a dream and wake up to find herself alone and afraid again. She blocked these thoughts from her mind.

"So, where exactly are we? I mean, what is this place?" she asked.

"Well, this is where Sam, Michael, Alex and I have been living since the night we all got split up," he told her. "We call it The Bunker, since it's underground.

"The Bunker?" Amelia asked, still amazed that this place even existed.

"Well, Sam hates the name, but in all honestly, you won't find many things she doesn't *dislike*," he laughed and then added, "don't tell her I said that. She'd kill me."

"I won't," said Amelia, earnestly. "She looks like she could kill *me* if I say much of anything."

Apollo laughed again. "Don't worry too much about her, she's just that way. She wants you to be intimidated, but deep down it's just a front. She's actually quite docile, once you get to know her."

"I'll take your word for it," she said. "This place is amazing. Was it always this way?"

"Yes, at least, ever since I can remember. When we arrived, everything was set up for us. The location was secret, only Alex and Finn were meant to know about it. Alex brought us here, after we all got split up. We waited for you and Finn to show up, but you never did. Alex never gave up hope, that one day you guys would return, until…"

"Until what?" Amelia asked.

"She told us that she knew Finn was dead," said Apollo.

"But… How? How did she know?"

Apollo shook his head. "To be honest, Alex kept a lot of things to herself. She always said she would tell us everything when we were old enough. After she knew about Finn, she pretty much dedicated every moment on getting you back. We all did."

"What happened to Alex? Is she – dead?"

"I can only hope she's not," said Apollo. "A little over three years ago, she told us that there might be a lead to finding you. Sam wanted to go with her, she practically begged her. Alex refused. She said she would be okay, that she needed Sam to stay here and look after us. To keep us safe in case anything went wrong. That she would be back before we knew it, but, she never came back. We had to keep going on our own."

"There are so many things I want to know," said Amelia. "I think I'll never stop asking you questions! It could become very annoying."

Apollo laughed. "Don't worry about it. I'm sure I'll have just as many questions for you. We have a few years to catch up on, after all."

"Did Alex ever tell you how this place was built? Where all this came from?"

"As we got older, we began to ask more and more questions. But, like I said, Alex was always very secretive, even with us. She never wanted to talk about how it was possible to have all these things. The one thing she did tell us, was how to restock our food and cash supply, if we ever needed to. There is an old storage unit and, every year we could go there and there was a new shipment of supplies, food, cash, clothes, new technology, pretty much everything you could need. That's how we managed to keep everything up to date, and how we replenished our food supply and money."

Amelia listened to his story in shock. This was something she would have never imagined. Who could possibly deliver these things for them all this time? How did they never find out where it all came from?

"Just like that? And you don't find that odd? I mean, didn't you ever wonder where it all came from?"

"Of course we did. Hell, I still wonder, to this day," he said. "But, we've never received any communication from anyone. Alex was the only link we had to any of it. She had contacts, she just never told us who they were. But we knew. After she disappeared, no one ever came here looking for us. It's like this place really did not exist to anyone but us."

"This is much nicer than what I had growing up…"

Apollo nodded. "I wish so many things could have been different, Ames. I truly do… But hey, you're here now, so let's make the most of it! Tomorrow morning, I'll give you the grand tour of The Bunker, get you feeling warm and cozy here in no time. We really do have a bit of everything."

"Thanks, that sounds great," she said.

There was a moment of silence between them. She usually felt awkward around people. If he picked up on it, he did not show it. She was grateful for this.

"You really don't remember anything? About us, or what happened when they came for us that night?"

Amelia shook her head. "I just remember being afraid and alone. I remember Finn telling me to hide, and to not move, no matter what. He told me he would come back for me… but he never did."

There was a moment of silence between them. Apollo reached out and took her hand. "I wish we would have all stayed together," he said. "Maybe things would have worked out differently."

"Or maybe we would all be dead or captured," she suggested.

"True… I guess there's really not much use wondering how things could have been."

"Not really," she said.

"Sam wants us all to talk," he told her. "Do you feel up to it?"

Amelia nodded. "Yes, I really want to understand more about what's going on."

"Okay, let's go."

CHAPTER FOUR

Apollo lead her to a room at the far back of The Bunker. In this room there were three 70" computer monitors lining the walls. The screens were showing different news broadcasts from around the city. One of them showed the fire that they had just left behind.

Samantha was sitting in front of the screens, typing commands on the keyboard that controlled them.

"What is this?" asked Amelia, sitting down in an empty chair next to Samantha.

"This is our security room," said Apollo. "Through the years, we've been able to update our systems and have managed to keep them as modern as possible. From here, we have always been monitoring any news that could have been caused by something unnatural. That's how we found you."

Amelia looked confused.

"I told you before, we've been trying to find you for years. Since the very first day we arrived, Alex was always monitoring the news, looking for signs of anything out of the ordinary. When she disappeared, we continued the search. We knew that your powers could be out of control at some point or that you would use them if you were in danger. If you caused enough damage it was meant to be broadcast somewhere."

"We've chased after hundreds of fires during the years with no luck," added Samantha.

"This time we got lucky," said Apollo.

"You have no idea how grateful I am for that," said Amelia.

"I don't know how much you remember about that night, but we need to know if Finn told you anything... Or left you anything that could help," said Samantha.

"What do you mean 'help'?" asked Amelia.

"Help finding Snyde," said Apollo.

"Who is Snyde?" asked Amelia. This was all getting a bit confusing.

"Didn't you wonder who those men were last night?" Samantha asked. "Why they were after you?"

Amelia felt a bit ashamed. She really had not given that much thought. Everything else that was going on around her now had taken all her attention.

"I just figured they were police officers," said Amelia.

"With heavy military weapons and armour?" Apollo asked, smiling.

"Never mind. Let's start from what we know," said Samantha. "The night we split up, Oleander Snyde sent his men after us, they wanted to capture all four of us, to continue their experiments. Experiments that our parents had participated in. They were part of a human enhancement project. Snyde Corp wanted to create human weapons, people with special abilities and powers that would be better than any weapon in the market."

"Wait, how is it that you know all of this?" Amelia interrupted.

"Because of this."

Samantha hit a few keys on the keyboard in front of her and pointed to the screen on her right.

A video began to play. In it, was a man sitting in a small dark room, staring directly at them. It was Finn. Amelia didn't think she would ever see his face again. She choked back tears that began to form as he began to speak.

"I'm recording this because I think you deserve to know the truth about where you come from. Alexa thinks it will only hurt you, but you must be prepared. This fight isn't over. They won't stop coming for you... Not until you're captured or dead."

Amelia stared in shock at the screen as Finn's message continued.

"The four of you were born in a facility, under Snyde Corps' control. They conducted top secret experiments, trying to create human weapons of destruction. Your parents were all a part of these experiments. At first, they didn't truly know what they had signed on for. They had been told they were to be test subjects for new medicines that could make the human body immune to any disease.

I was one of the scientists assigned to their experiments. After some time, I began to realize what the experiments were actually for. Snyde wanted to create weapons, to give humans abilities to control different elements, to be able to use these abilities in open combat. The ability to control fire, electricity, air and water.

All their test subjects were also induced with regenerative capabilities. The subjects would heal much quicker than any normal human. When you were born, the serums that your parents had been given somehow affected you. All these abilities had been passed on and you developed these gifts naturally. They were a part of your DNA.

The experiments weren't going as planned. All of the subjects eventually began to reject the serums. They were deteriorating. But the four of you were not. Your abilities were perfect. You had been born with them, so they were a part of you. There was no rejection. Snyde wanted to start a new experiment, using your DNA to create new versions of the serums... Some that other humans wouldn't reject. When I heard of this, I knew I couldn't let that happen. You were only children. I decided to break you out of the facility. Alexa and I created a plan to get you out. We were successful, but we knew that someday they would come looking for you.

You have to be ready when they do. You have to learn to use your powers. To be more powerful than anything Snyde can send after you. I don't know if I will always be there to help you. But if I'm not, I need you to stick together. You will be a stronger force if you're together. Trust each other, rely on one another and always remember all the sacrifices that have been made to keep you safe.

I'm sorry that I put you through all of this. I hope one day you will forgive me. If I'm not there to guide you, please forgive me."

The screen went blank. Amelia was trying to process all this information and make sense of it. These powers had been the cause of an experiment. Her parents had been a part of it. Parents she had never met. People that chose to be part of some madness instead of being a part of her life. She again fought back tears that were forming. She didn't even know if they were tears of sadness or anger.

"Are you okay?" asked Apollo.

"Where's Michael?" Amelia asked suddenly, as if only just having processed that he was not here in the Bunker with them.

Samantha's demeanour seemed to change at the question. "Mikey was taken."

"Taken?" asked Amelia.

"By Snyde Corp," added Apollo. "They've had him for almost a year now," Apollo walked over to Samantha and put his hand reassuringly on her shoulder. "We need to get him back, we're just not sure where to start."

"Those are the same people that came after me last night?" Amelia asked.

"Yes," said Apollo. "Those men were part of Snyde Corp, working under Oleander Snyde's orders. He wants us, to use our DNA and perfect his experiments."

"Did Finn ever mention anything to you about where Snyde Corp could be?" Samantha asked, hopefully. "Is there anything you remember that can help?"

"I – I really don't know," Amelia stuttered slightly. "I can't remember much about that night. I don't even remember hearing the name before."

"Is there anything you *do* remember?" asked Apollo, gently.

Amelia closed her eyes in concentration. "I remember running... Finn telling me to run faster... it was raining and we ran to an old building... On to the roof. He told me to hide and no matter what I heard to stay hidden."

"Then what?"

"I hid... And I heard footsteps – and gunshots, but I couldn't see anything," continued Amelia. "I could hear Finn's voice... but it sounded far away and muffled. Then I didn't hear anything anymore. I stayed hidden all night. I fell asleep in my hiding spot. The next morning, I woke up and I was still alone. He had never come back for me. I waited there for a couple of days, scared that they would be waiting for me when I got out. I began to grow hungry, so I decided to take off on my own."

"You don't remember anything else?" Samantha insisted. "Finn didn't say anything else to you?"

"No, nothing... Sorry, but I was too young and scared. I can't remember."

Samantha looked annoyed but said nothing else.

"That's alright," said Apollo. "It's not your fault, we wouldn't know much either, if it wasn't for the few things Alex shared, this place or this video Finn left. You have nothing to be sorry for, truly."

Amelia nodded appreciatively. If only Samantha was as understandable as Apollo. She had the impression that Samantha didn't like her all that much. She wasn't even giving her a chance to get to know her.

Samantha got up, took something out of her pocket and handed it to Apollo.

"I took this off one of our friends last night," she said. "It looks like a small comms device. See if you can get anything from it. Maybe it can come in handy."

Apollo looked at the small device. It was a tiny radio, much smaller than any mobile phone or walkie talkie. "Great, I'll see if I can get it to work and maybe we can tap into their frequency. Get information from anything they send through other devices."

"Do what you can," said Samantha, she gave Apollo a warm smile. "Any new lead is better than nothing."

"What can I do to help?" asked Amelia.

"First, you have to learn how to control your powers," Samantha told her. "You're a danger to yourself and everyone around you until you do. Tomorrow we'll start training."

"Will *you* be training me?" Amelia asked, timidly.

"Yes, I'll be training you... Unless you have a problem with that."

"No, of course not!"

"Good, I'll see you tomorrow... Bright and early."

Samantha walked out of the room. Apollo took a seat in front of the computer and began examining the device immediately.

"Okay, it's official. She hates me," said Amelia.

Apollo started laughing. "Don't worry about Sam, really! She doesn't hate you."

"Easy for you to say, she's all smiles with you!"

Apollo blushed a little and looked away. "She's just a bit tough, but she doesn't hate you. Trust me."

"Maybe you're just a bit biased with her," she said. "I swear, I'm afraid she'll slap me at any moment."

Apollo laughed again. "She will warm up to you eventually, although, I have told her she needs to work on her people skills."

"That's putting it lightly... Is there anything I can do to help with that?" she pointed to the small comms device.

"No, don't worry about it. I'll be okay. You get some rest."

CHAPTER FIVE

After two hours scanning the news and checking the communication device Samantha had retrieved, Apollo felt he had hit a dead end. There wasn't much more he could do here. He leaned back in his chair, closed his eyes and took a deep breath. He was exhausted. So much had happened in the past days. They had finally made progress. Last night was a success in what had been years of loses for them.

He sat for a few more minutes before deciding to go for a swim at the downstairs pool. One of his favourite pastimes. The feel of the water helped him relax. Nothing else mattered when he was in the water.

He made his way down to the second floor and was walking towards the pool when he noticed the lights on at the back of the hall. The lights leading to their training room. Knowing that Samantha was probably in there setting up for tomorrow's training session with Amelia, he decided to make a small detour and check up on her.

Apollo opened the door gently, trying his best not to disturb her. Upon entering this room there was a control booth, with a main panel created to program simulations in order to assist with training. Enemies, hazards and obstacles of all types could be programmed. Some were very realistic, some could cause serious harm if the person practicing became careless.

The point of having these options was to better prepare them for the real threat. That's what Alex had told them. She had closely monitored every training session they had ever had. Making sure they never got in over their heads. Each of them had practiced at different levels of difficulty.

For Michael, it had all been an amazing, fun videogame, always set to the highest difficulty. His obstacles consisted of armed attackers, challenging him to become stronger and faster. For Samantha, it had always been about the discipline. She was always focused and one step ahead of the simulations. Her focus was on how to outsmart her opponents, with higher levels of stealth. For Apollo, he had simply seen it as a way to prepare his mind. His simulations created puzzles, challenging him to think of ways to go around obstacles and opponents, not facing the danger directly.

Beyond the main control booth was the training room. The size of an airplane hangar with walls of thick concrete and steel. Ropes, steps, climbing walls, ramps, sandbags, crevices, metal spikes, all covered the area.

He stood in front of the panel and looked through the thick glass separating it from the rest of the hangar. He stared out disapprovingly. Samantha was not setting up for Amelia, she was having a late night session of her own. And she had not taken it easy on the difficulty. He watched as the simulation played out.

She stood in the centre of the hangar, surrounded by at least three dozen holographic soldiers, each taking shots at her. Even with his disapproval, he could not help but be impressed at her ease of dispatching each soldier. One by one they disintegrated into thin air as she struck them with electric charges. With each soldier she took out, more regenerated.

He looked on at her, his disapproval increasing with each new figure that appeared.

This is stupid, what is she trying to prove? He thought.

After a few minutes, one of the soldiers connected a shot and Samantha was thrust backwards. He had a sudden urge to barge in, but he watched on.

Samantha turned and aimed a shot of her own at the soldier and it vanished in a poof of yellow dust. Then, another soldier connected a shot. The pain that came from each impact from the holograms was quite intense. It sent a surge of energy straight into your body, paralysing its target for a second. After the second soldier hit, another struck and then another.

He couldn't take it anymore. Apollo hit a few buttons on the main panel and the simulation shut down, plunging the hangar into temporary darkness, before the lights flickered back on to their normal state.

Samantha looked around and noticed him for the first time since he had come into the room.

"What did you do that for?" she asked, glaring at him through narrow eyes.

He walked towards her shaking his head.

"What do yo mean? Are you serious?" Apollo asked. "I wasn't too keen on watching you take enough hits to make you pass out."

"I was more than capable of handling that," she said.

She walked past him and reached for a water bottle and a towel. He watched as she wiped the sweat from her face and took a sip from her water.

"Do you want to talk about it? Or would you prefer I just leave you to it until you hurt yourself?"

She did not answer or look at him. He pressed on.

"Honestly, Sam, what is going on with you? I thought you would be elated we finally found Amelia. That we managed to get her back."

Samantha ran her hands through her hair in frustration.

"Look, Polo, maybe that's just it," she said, exasperatedly.

He looked confused. "I'm not sure I understand."

"It's just, we found her," said Samantha. "We managed to do what Alex couldn't. We got her back. So, now what?"

He still felt confused. Unsure of the real problem.

"Now, we help her train," he said. "We keep on preparing."

"I know that, Polo... But, *then* what?"

"I don't think I'm following," said Apollo.

She took a deep breath, trying to keep her tone calm.

"All this time, we've had something do," said Samantha. "We've been tracking fires, trying to find her. Now, we've found her... And there is nothing more to track. We have nowhere else to go... We don't have any leads or any place to start looking for Mikey, or even Alex, if they're even —"

"They're alive, Sam," he said. "I know they are."

She nodded, unconvincingly. He walked over to her and pulled her into a hug.

"Listen, I promise you," he said. "No matter what, we will find them. We will get Mike back. Even if we don't have anything to go on now, I know we can find something. Somewhere. But, for now, let's focus on helping Amelia. She needs us."

"I know," she said. "Thanks, Polo. Sorry for being so snappy lately. I don't know what I would do without you. You know that, don't you?"

"That's something you won't have to worry about," he said.

They left the training room together. It was too late for his swim now, so they took the elevator back to the main floor. They stopped in front of Samantha's room to say goodnight.

"So, tomorrow morning, I'm going to take Amelia for a short tour of The Bunker," he said. "I figured it would help her get used to her surroundings. Feel more comfortable here."

"Good idea," said Samantha. "Just don't keep her too long. You tend to talk a lot."

He smiled. "I'll have her ready by 11:00."

"Great," said Samantha.

He turned to walk towards his own room when she called back to him.

"Polo?"

"Hmm?" He turned to look at her.

"Thanks, again. For everything."

"Not a problem," he said. "Just try to get some sleep."

"You know me," she said. "I don't get much sleep."

"Just give it a try. It might help you see things better tomorrow."

She nodded and stepped into her room. He looked back at her closed door before slowly walking into his.

CHAPTER SIX

Amelia wasn't able to get much sleep that night. She was exhausted, and her head was spinning with so much new information. For the most part, she had hated her powers. They scared her, brought her grief and had done nothing more than cause her misery.

She had always wished she didn't have them. She wanted to be as normal as any other person. And now, finally, she knew why it was this way. Her parents had been part of an experiment. *She* was just a product of the same experiments. How could they have agreed to this? Not considering what the consequences or side effects might be. Even if they had not known the true reason for the experiment, how could they have stayed after they had found it out. She was angry, upset and sad all at the same time.

She closed her eyes to try to sleep but all she did was think. Images kept creeping in on her thoughts. She tried to focus on those images. Images of a dark rainy night, long ago. Memories. Maybe memories that she hadn't thought of in so many years, had never given any importance to them. Now, she was being questioned about them. She felt it was important to remember or at least she had to try.

She tried to focus on details about that night. She remembered running, Finn by her side, egging her to run faster, to not look back. They reached the building, he knelt beside her and told her to hide. She couldn't remember his exact words, everything was too blurry. She was angry with herself, for not remembering more.

She sat up in her bed, feeling angry and foolish at the same time. What difference did any of this make? She didn't know anything that could possibly help anyone. She didn't know anything at all. All she knew was how to run and hide. It was the one thing she had done her entire life. It felt wrong to be here, with a warm bed to sleep in, food on the table, clean clothes and shelter. She couldn't help but feel that all this was a dream and that tomorrow, she would wake up and all of it would be gone.

She lay back down and forced herself to close her eyes once more. This time, sleep crept in, finally taking over and she felt herself slowly drifting in and out of consciousness, until at last, she was fast asleep.

****

Two deafening shots were fired, and one man dropped to the floor, lifeless. Oleander Snyde walked over the dead man's body and turned to face another man who was trying his hardest to remain calm and not beg for his life.

"How is it that, with all the resources I have provided you over the years, you still failed?" Snyde asked the man, his voice almost a whisper. "They were all there for the taking, and yet, they slipped through your fingers once more."

The man didn't dare speak.

Snyde pointed his gun directly at the man's face. "I recommend you think of an answer… A good one. A lot depends on your choice of words."

"Sir – I – they were just –" the man's voice was shaking.

"What? They were what?" asked Snyde, his voice challenging.

"They were… too powerful, sir. We were no match for their abilities. We tried, but –"

Another gun shot was fired and the fell, his lifeless body contorted on the floor. Snyde walked out of the room, not once glancing at the two men whose lives he had just ended. He walked up to a woman standing guard in front of the door.

"Take care of that mess," he pointed to the room he had just exited. He continued walking down corridor after corridor, until coming to a large metal door with an electric lock, operated by a hand and retina scanner.

Only two people had access to this room. He placed his hand and eye for the scanner and stepped inside. This room contained a dozen other metal doors, six on each side of the corridor and each one secured by its own individual electric lock. Snyde stopped in front of the third door on his right. He scanned his hand and the door slid open.

Inside the room was a young man, he was on his knees, his arms stretched on either side by two enormous chains. His entire body showed signs of torture and malnourishment. When Snyde stepped into the room, the young man looked up slowly and managed a weak smile.

"How nice of you to visit," he said, sarcastically. "It gets awfully lonely down here."

Snyde didn't reply. He just stared at the young man. Michael Clarke had received daily torture since he had been captured, and yet he had said nothing about the others, never given away their whereabouts, never revealing any weakness. Snyde had to admire his resilience and strength. There was no way to break him and yet he had decided not to kill him… At least not yet. There were still other uses for him.

"I just thought I would pay you a visit to update you on your friends," said Snyde.

Michael pulled on his restraints. "If you hurt them – "

"I'm sure there's not much you can do to stop me," Snyde retorted with a smile. He enjoyed seeing the pain in his prisoner's face. "You are nothing without your powers, so don't make empty threats, boy."

"Why don't you take these chains off and we'll see how much damage I can do, even without my powers," growled Michael.

Snyde walked closer to Michael, stopping at his side and grabbing him roughly by his hair. He pulled his head back as Michael struggled, unable to loosen Snyde's strong grip. "I will kill you and every person you care about in this world, but in the meantime, you will continue to be useful to me and my experiments."

He pulled a long syringe from his pocket and plunged it directly into Michael's neck, draining a sample of his blood and then releasing him.

"That should be enough for now." Snyde pursed his lips into a malevolent smile. "You have no idea how much you are helping with my new creation. I'll make sure to test him on you before sending him out on his first field assignment."

Michael struggled agains't his restraints, tugging and pulling until he was out of breath. The skin on his wrists bleeding raw from his efforts. "I swear, one day I'll make you pay for everything you've done!" he yelled at Snyde.

Snyde simply gave him a dry smile and walked out of the room.

CHAPTER SEVEN

The following morning, Amelia woke with a start. She had been having dreams – nightmares really, but could not quite remember what they had been about. A part of her thought that being in a safe place would have stopped the constant nightmares. It was not the case.

For as long as she could remember the dreams had been a part of her life. Last night there had been a woman's voice. She couldn't remember what the woman was saying, but her voice was dark and sinister, like a person with no soul had been speaking to her.

She looked at the clock on her bedside table. It was only 6:30 in the morning, she should try to get more sleep. The moment she had closed her eyes again there was a loud knock and her door swung open. Amelia jumped out of bed in shock.

"Time to get up!" said Apollo, a little too cheerful for her taste. "Oh, you're already up! That's great. Hope you had a good night's sleep."

"Hardly," Amelia mumbled and lay back down.

He walked to the bed and pulled her up into a sitting position. "Well, there will be plenty of time for sleep later," he said, too enthusiastically. "I'll wait for you outside while you get ready, and then we can start."

"Start?" Amelia was still too tired to function correctly.

"Yes, we can start that tour I told you about," he said. "So, you can see everything The Bunker has to offer. Then, later today I'll have to hand you over to Sam, for your first training session."

Amelia gasped slightly. This was more intimidating than anything else she had faced. Just the thought of how disappointed Samantha would be with her abilities made her cringe.

Apollo appeared to know exactly what was going through her mind. He laughed.

"It won't be that bad," he said. "Come on, get ready and we can get an early start."

He left the room and she got up, quickly brushed her teeth and found something to wear. The closet in her room had a small selection of jeans and shirts for her to change into. Even though there wasn't too much variety, she was grateful to have options. It had been a while since she had slept on such a comfortable bed and woken up to having a choice of what to wear or hot food.

In ten minutes she was ready and met Apollo just outside her room.

"Ready?" He asked.

"As I'll ever be," she smiled.

"Perfect," he said, smiling back.

Something about him was so comforting. He acted as though no time had gone by, or like they had been friends all their lives. Not separated for ten years.

"Well, starting with this main hallway," said Apollo, spreading his arms out, pointing to their current surroundings. "You have all our main bedrooms. That there, three doors down from your room, is Sam's room."

"So, that's the one to stay away from?" she asked, making a mental note.

"Precisely." He laughed. "Right next door to yours is my room. No need to stay away from that one. If you ever need anything, you can just knock on the wall and I'll come running."

She nodded, gratefully. At least with Apollo here, she would definitely feel a bit more relaxed and at home.

"Further along the hall, turn the corner and on your right, that's Michael's room," he said. "Since he was taken, nothing in that room has been changed. It will be there waiting for him when he gets back."

"Can I ask, how was he taken?"

Apollo put his hands behind his neck, looking a bit uncomfortable. "To be honest, I would rather have Sam tell that story. It's sort of a sensitive topic."

"Oh… okay, sorry," she said. "I didn't mean to intrude."

"No, don't worry about it," he said. "It's not a secret or anything. It's just, Mikey got caught trying to protect Sam. She's taken it pretty hard. She has never given much detail about what happened. But, I know we'll get him back someday soon. I really do."

Amelia nodded. "Hey, you managed to find me. I'm sure we can find him as well."

"Me too," he said. "But, let's not lose track of our tour, please. I have been practicing my speech all night, you know?"

She laughed. She hardly recognized her own laughter anymore, it was like it came from a stranger. The last time she had laughed felt like a lifetime away. It was a good feeling.

"There are two unused rooms," Apollo continued. "One of them was Alex's and then there was a room meant for Finn. But, you know… He never made it back."

He cleared his throat and signalled her to follow him. At the end of the hall, they stopped in front of a small elevator.

"How big is this place?" Amelia asked, not understanding the need for an elevator in an underground hideout.

"You'll be surprised," he said. "The Bunker has four floors. The living room, kitchen, security room and bedrooms, which you have already seen, are all on the first floor. The three remaining floors are all lower underground. The next floor down has our library, training room, pool area and food storage. Then, the third floor down has a lab area, medical bay and weapons armoury. The last floor has – wait for it – our very own movie theatre. That's where we'll end the tour and then meet up with Sam for your first session."

"Are you serious?"

She could not believe what she was hearing. This place had everything a person could need and more. Medical bay? Weapons Armory? Movie theatre? She would never have imagined this in a million years.

"Not wanting to sound repetitive, but how is this place even possible?"

Apollo shrugged his shoulders. "Listen, we were even more shocked than you when we first started discovering everything this place had. Even Alex was as surprised as we were by some of the things the facility had to offer. Finn was the one who took care of the design, so there were some surprises, even for her. Little by little we started learning more and more, about the computer systems, security systems, Alex helped us get educated with all the thousands of books in the library. After being here for a month, she decided it was a good idea to enrol us in school, so that we could interact with other kids our age. But, we always had to be extra careful, not to give anything away about who we really were, and what we were capable of.

It wasn't always that easy. Most of all for Michael. He always was one to boast and brag. He hated having to keep his abilities secret."

Amelia listened to everything in amazement. She knew that it had been hard on them, no matter what the circumstances. Even though she had been alone, with nothing or no one to help her, she understood that it had not been easy for the other three either, but she could not help but feel a bit jealous at all they had growing up. Especially the fact that they had had a parental figure, to look after them, keep them safe and care for them.

"Finn and Alex set this whole place up for us," said Apollo. "So, we could all live here together. Things just didn't work out like they planned."

There were so many questions going through Amelia's mind now. It all seemed so sudden. Just hours ago she had been running, seeking shelter in an abandoned barn, now she was standing in some kind of safe-house, with all the luxuries she had always lacked, with people who knew her yet she could not remember. She looked at Apollo, who stared back, not saying anything more.

Not knowing what else to say at the moment, she pressed her finger against the small button to signal the elevator. When the doors opened they both stepped inside. Apollo hit the the indicator for the third floor.

"Like I said before, everything is underground," he said. "The ground floor is really the fourth floor, then it goes all the way down to the first."

Amelia nodded, but still did not speak. She could sense him eyeing her, perhaps wondering what was going through her mind. She did not really know what to think, so many things were muddled. She should have a million questions, yet nothing came to mind. As if he knew could read her thoughts, he spoke.

"You can ask me anything you want, Ames. I know it's hard to trust us," he paused for a moment, "but, we really do want you to feel as comfortable as possible."

"I know," she said. "I'm sorry if I seem too quiet, it's just hard to get my head around everything that's happened in the past day."

He smiled. "I can only imagine… How about for now, we move on with the tour?"

"That would be great."

He led her out of the elevator and into a huge open space, with three giant sliding doors. He pointed to the first door on their right.

"This is our main food storage," he said, jovially. "When we first found this room, there was enough food to last for five years. Or at least, that's what we calculated. All none perishable goods. Want to have a look?"

He led her into the room. She gasped at what she saw. Countless shelves on all sides of the room, stocked up with all kinds of foods. Canned goods, dried foods, cereals, sauces, sweets occupied the shelves. At the back she spotted large freezers. When they walked closer Apollo pointed out frozen processed meats, dairy, pizzas, ice creams.

"After the initial supply, Alex would always drive to the secret storage area I told you about and pick up whatever was delivered."

"I'm sorry," said Amelia. "I just can't understand, how it's possible that she never mentioned anything about where this all came from. I mean, she had to know. It was clear she was in contact with someone."

"I know," he said. "Trust me, you have no idea how foolish we feel about it. We must have asked her a thousand times. Sam was the oldest, so she tried hardest to get as much information out of her as possible. Alex was always so secretive. She would just avoid it, tell us that she would tell us more when we were old enough to understand everything. You have no idea the amount of arguments this caused between Alex and Sam. Their personalities clashed a little, and this always detonated major confrontations. Sam even threatened to leave the Bunker a few times."

"Really?"

Apollo nodded. "Alex wanted us to be in this bubble, protected from everything. I guess, I know why she wanted to protect us, but I don't think keeping us in the dark was the best way to do so."

"This is crazy," she said.

"Anyhow, at least you won't go hungry if you stick with us, that's for sure," he said.

After seeing all there was in this room, they walked back into the open hall.

"Next up, the library," said Apollo. "You will literally find books on anything and everything in here. It could take you a while to find it, though. It is a bit spacious."

When he opened the doors, she immediately understood what he meant. Spacious was an understatement. If the food storage had impressed her, it was nothing compared to how she felt at seeing this. Countless rows of books, one after the other. There must have been thousands – if not millions – of books here. She walked towards the first few rows and saw even more rows as she grew closer. Her mouth hung open, her eyes transfixed on all the different volumes. Science, maths, english literature, sociology, cooking, anything she could think of, it was here.

"If you want, you can choose one to take with you for late night reading," he said.

"Reading?" Amelia asked, not really listening to what he had said.

"Er, yes… You do know *how* to read, don't you?" he asked, rather shyly.

"What? Of course I do," she said, defensively.

"Hey, I didn't mean anything by it," he raised his hands up in the air. "It's just, you know… I'm just checking."

Amelia rolled her eyes at him. As she continued to look at the books she found one that caught her attention.

"Can I take this one?" she asked.

"Little Women? Great choice," he said. "Come on, let's keep going. We need to hurry up, or else we'll be late for you first training session."

She felt a knot tighten in her stomach. She had almost forgotten. The thought of training made her somewhat nauseous. She felt like she had swallowed a brick. Of course, it could just be the fact that Samantha would train her. That was already intimidating enough. Add the fact that she had never had any real control over her abilities and that she was bound to disappoint, it was enough to make her want to run away from this new found sanctuary.

After the library, Apollo showed her the gym, which included many different types of exercise machinery, the pool house and pointed to the door in the back that lead to the training room. Then, they went down to the lower floor. He led her to the medical wing. Surgical equipment, that he admitted none of them knew how to use since they all had healing abilities, they had never had any need for it.

"One time, Mikey was trying to show off and set his training program to expert. It was way more than he could handle, and he wound up with a huge arrow in his stomach," said Apollo. "As soon as we removed the arrow, blood was sprayed everywhere. By the time we brought him down here, he had all but healed."

"Is that the – umm – the same training program *I'm* going to be using?

Apollo laughed. "No, don't worry about it. I mean, you could use it if you wanted to, but it's not what Sam has planned for you. He was using the attack simulations. Thinking he was the toughest guy out there. Being stupid and reckless, if you ask me. But, that's how he is."

Amelia nodded. "Can I ask you something?"

"Sure, what's on your mind?"

"Why the training? I mean, what is it we're preparing for?"

"We mentioned Snyde Corp before," said Apollo. "Even though we've managed to stay hidden all these years, what Finn said was right. They will not stop looking for us, and we have to be prepared when the time finally comes."

"But, he surely won't be able to find us here," said Amelia. "I mean, you guys have been here for ten years."

"I know, but look at what's happened," said Apollo. "We've lost two people already. Even though this place has not been compromised, we can't guarantee it never will. Oleander Snyde runs Snyde Corp. He will never stop looking for us. He wants our DNA, the secret to our powers. Why we are the way we are. If he has that, there's no telling what he will do."

A new fear crept into Amelia. The fear of being forever hunted. Of not being able to be safe, no matter where she went. And now, the fear of not being able to master her abilities enough to be of any use to the others. What if she was no good and they decided they could not have her around? If they gave up on her too easily?

"It's a lot to take in," said Apollo. "I promise we'll talk more about it later. But, for now I suggest we hurry downstairs, check out the movie theatre and then come back to the training room, or else you will really upset Sam. She's going to be waiting, all ready for your very first session."

"Sounds amazing," said Amelia, sarcastically. She felt her mouth go dry. Suddenly she had the feeling of having eaten cotton balls for breakfast. "I can't wait to hear her pep talks."

Apollo offered her a wide grin. "They are all inspiring. Now, come on. It will be better if you don't think about it too much. Just get in there and do you best."

CHAPTER EIGHT

As she waited for the doors to open into her impending doom, she could not help but think that, between last night's uneasy dreams and this morning's first training session, this may well be the day she dies. It wasn't easy for her to use her powers, in fact, if it were up to her she would never use them again. But now, they were forcing her to learn, egging her on to use the one thing that had brought her so much grief and destruction. If only they knew what they were asking of her. All the pain in her past.

She shook these thoughts out and took a few deep breaths. *Ready as I'll ever be,* she thought. She looked at Apollo, his face was relaxed, even joyful. Of course, it wasn't him making his way to the slaughter house.

"Are you nervous?"

"Not really," she lied, looking at her hands.

"It's okay if you're a bit apprehensive about this, you know? I'm not here to judge you."

"Were you ever nervous when you started training?"

"Me? I was sooo worried about never being able to fully control my powers," he said, sincerely. "To be honest, I still feel like there are many aspects of my abilities that I still have to develop. Sam's always telling me I should push myself a bit more, that she knows there's more to me hidden somewhere."

"It's easier for you though, your powers can't destroy the whole house like mine can... you can't risk hurting someone you care about as badly as I can."

He stepped out and looked at her. His face was serious, lacking his usual grin. She stopped, a bit ashamed of what she had said. She didn't want him to think she was undermining his abilities. He was the one of the nicest people she had ever met, and probably the closest thing to a friend she had come to find in a long time.

"I'm sorry… I didn't mean to offend you or upset you. I'm just –" she stopped mid-sentence, not sure really what she wanted to say.

"You didn't, it just reminded me of what Michael used to say about my powers. He thought my abilities were 'too much defence, not enough offense'. That's how he always put it. But, I have the ability to literally remove all air from a person's body. I could easily harm someone if I'm not careful. Besides, I have the power to create mighty hurricanes that could ravage cities."

Amelia stared at him in shock.

"Can you really do that?" she asked, in awe.

Apollo laughed. "Not sure, but I supposed I should be able to. I've never had a go at it."

Amelia rolled her eyes and smiled.

"I'm just saying, I know how important it is to learn control," he said. "We all need to be aware of the damage we could do if we were to lose control of our abilities."

"I'll bet Sam never has to worry about losing control," she rolled her eyes, thinking about how emotionless Samantha appeared to be.

"Don't be too sure," he said softly. "She's just very good at hiding her emotions. She tries very hard to always be in control. That doesn't mean she has no worries. She has always been afraid of what would happen if our powers ever fall into the wrong hands…"

"Are you two really going to stand out here in the hallway and have a nice chat all day?" Samantha's voice called from a door at the end of the hall.

Apollo smiled sideways at Amelia. "Looks like we'll have to finish this some other time. Training awaits."

He opened the door and guided her inside. As soon as she stepped in, Amelia found herself more than intimidated. The training room's size was the first thing to impress her. She was sure you could have comfortably fit four airplanes here. Then, there were all sorts of obstacles set out across different spaces.

Samantha was standing behind the large control panel with a computer screen and different buttons and levers, right at the front of the room.

Apollo whispered "good luck" to Amelia as they approached her.

"You have no idea how much I appreciate you being late," she began. "It really shows me that you will be taking this very seriously."

"It was my fault, Sam," said Apollo, winking at Amelia. "I distracted her with my excessive talking. You know how it is. It won't happen again."

"Let's just get started, shall we?" She looked at Amelia for confirmation, who in return nodded her head slightly.

She was suddenly feeling very sick to her stomach and they hadn't even told her what she would work on. She could feel a fire deep down, trying to burst free from her nerves. She fought as hard as she could against it, balling her hands into fists and digging her finger nails into her palms. This worked sometimes, when trying to keep her powers in check, but no foolproof way of controlling it.

"Take a few minutes and tell me what you see," said Samantha.

Was this a trick question? Should she answer that she saw ropes and sandbags? Climbing walls? Whatever she said, she was sure she would be wrong, so why not take a wild guess.

"Training equipment?" she ventured a guess.

"Clearly... Not exactly what I was after." Samantha pointed at the ceiling. "Take a better look."

All around the ceiling, perched on wooden ledges high above were candles. Not just a few of them, but hundreds and hundreds of candles.

"So, for your first training I wanted to start you off with something simple. I want you to focus on lighting each and every one of those candles, without causing damage to the wooden ledges and without melting the wax. Just light the actual wick."

"That's supposed to be simple?" asked Amelia, aghast.

"It is simple, you just have to focus."

"That's easier said than done most of the time," she added, overwhelmed by the idea of this task.

"I have an idea," said Apollo. "We'll leave you alone to try and that way you won't feel the pressure of us watching. We can come back in a couple of hours."

Samantha did not look too convinced by this idea, but Apollo had already taken her hand and was dragging her out of the room.

****

"Let's give her some space," said Apollo, once they were out of earshot.

"We don't have time to give her space! She is so far behind in knowing and understanding her powers," said Samantha. She ran her hands through her hair, something she did often when frustrated.

"Just give her a chance. I agree, her situation is not ideal, but she is one of us. I believe we can help her... I definitely know that if anyone can teach her, it's you."

"Flattery is not going to calm me down," said Samantha, but deep down she felt a bit more relaxed. Apollo always had that effect on people, sometimes she thought it must be a part of his abilities. "Can we at least go and watch her progress in the security cameras?"

"That's probably a good idea," agreed Apollo. "That will give us an idea of her actual level and what she needs to improve on."

****

How do they expect me to do this? Amelia thought to herself as she stood in the middle of the hangar. 'You just have to focus', easy for her to say, she wasn't the one who had to go against everything that felt natural to her.

Fear and doubt crept in as she stood there. Without warning, the wooden ledge directly to her right caught fire and exploded off the wall. She let out a scream and jumped back. Flames shot out of her hands without any control and collided against the back wall.

She wanted to stop, but once her powers got started there was no way for her to instantly shut them off. All the wooden ledges began to catch fire. She closed her eyes tightly and tried to calm down. *Make it stop,* she repeated in her mind. *Just make it go away.* Fear was consuming her, losing any possibility of controlling the situation. The fire was beginning to spread. It was too fierce. Amelia backed up and put her arms around her body in defeat.

Water started to pour from tiny sprinklers lining the ceiling. The water was freezing cold, drenching her while slowly dousing the flames. As quickly as the sprinklers had begun, they stopped. Amelia gasped and shivered from the cold water, her clothes and hair soaked completely through. She stormed out of the training room, fuming, feeling humiliated and afraid. As she made her way down the hallway she walked straight into Apollo and Samantha. The force caused her to fall on her back. This moment could not get more embarrassing.

"Ames, are you okay?" asked Apollo.

Amelia could see he tried hard not to laugh, but she saw no comedy in the situation as water dripped down her face and mixed with her tears. A big puddle of water was forming around where she lay on the floor.

Apollo offered a hand to help her up, but she waived it away.

"Are – you – *seriously* – asking – me – that – question?" Her voice sounded high and squeaky. She sobbed as she spoke each word.

She got to her feet and glared at both of them. She looked ready to explode at any minor provocation, so the others remained quiet and let her speak her mind.

"The two of you just think all of this is so easy! It's like a game to you, well it's not that way for me! My whole life I've been alone, scared out of my mind at these *abilities*… its more like a curse to me and you expect me to want to use this – this *disease* that grew inside of me! I HATE THESE POWERS… I DON'T WANT TO USE THEM… I DON'T EVEN WANT TO HAVE THEM…" She took a deep breath before continuing while the others just stared.

"I JUST WANT TO BE NORMAL – TO BE LEFT ALONE!" she shouted, ran towards the elevator and disappeared from sight.

****

"That went really well, don't you think?" asked Apollo.

"Fantastically," Samantha answered. "I'll go talk to her."

"Are you sure that's a good idea? She seems rather sensitive at the moment."

"Maybe it's time she toughened up and grew up."

"That's a harsh thing to say, even for you."

Samantha knew he was right, but she her annoyance at Amelia's lack of maturity and commitment drove her words.

"I know, but reality is harsh most of the time. These powers are not going to go away, no matter what she does. If she can't control them, then she will be a danger to herself and everyone around her."

Samantha walked to Amelia's room and knocked on the door. There was no answer, so she made her way in uninvited. Amelia was sitting on her bed, wiping tears from her eyes.

"Can we talk?"

"Do I have any choice?"

"You always do. We don't want to force you into this, no matter what you think. But, we will try to guide you so you can decide on what's best for you."

Amelia said nothing.

"Fine, I'll do all the talking. You can listen," said Samantha, rather harshly, more than she had intended. "Whether you like it or not this is your reality. You can try to run or hide from it but, sooner or later it will catch up to you. Your abilities will *not* go away and the more you reject them, the more dangerous they will become. I am leaving it to you. You can train and learn to control them or leave, because I will not have you endanger Polo and myself due to your serious lack of judgement."

Amelia looked at her for the first time since she had come into the room. "You're kicking me out?" Her voice trembled.

"No, I'm just giving you your options. Whatever happens is up to you."

"That's not fair!"

"It's fair enough. The choices we make lead us down the paths we want for ourselves, this is no different. If you want help we can give it to you, if you want to be left alone, then that's what you'll get." Samantha paused for a minute. She did not want to be the bad guy in this situation, she tried to soften her tone a bit. "Believe it or not, I know what you're going through."

"From what I've just heard, I really don't think you do."

"You think you're the only one who's had a tough time? That we haven't lost the people we care about? That we haven't had to live in hiding?"

"At least you had each other! You had Alex! And you had at least a partial taste of a normal life! You went to school, had friends! And this place! I had no one, not one person to care for me or to help me out, and then –"

"And then what?" Samantha asked, her voice harsh once more. "You think it's easy, having friends that you need to push away, worried that if you slip up someone could be watching? That one false move will get you found out? Knowing that you are being hunted is no more fun than being alone."

She did not have patience for this. This discussion was clearly not heading anywhere, and she was not going to waste her time.

"Tomorrow morning, we can continue training," said Samantha, calmly. "If you choose to give it another shot I will be there to help you, otherwise, you are free to go and do as you wish."

She turned around and exited the room leaving Amelia to consider her options.

CHAPTER NINE

Amelia sat alone in her room for what felt like hours, just thinking about what she was feeling. It was a mixture of anger, fear, despair and helplessness. This was too much to bear on her own. She badly wanted someone to talk to. That was something she had always wanted, and perhaps this was the first time in a long time that she felt like there was someone who would listen.

She dried her tears and left her room in search of Apollo. At least, she felt he would listen to her fears, not judge her. And he would hopefully not ask her to choose between difficult and impossible.

She first stopped by his room and softly rapped her knuckles against his door. No answer.

Alright, no problem. She thought.

Where could she check next? From their tour this morning she knew how big The Bunker actually was. This could take a while. She headed towards the elevator and pressed the button. She was startled when she heard her name called out.

"Amelia, do you need something?"

She spun around and saw Samantha leaning against the door to her room.

"Oh, I – no… not really," mumbled Amelia.

"Are you looking for Polo? I heard you knocking on his door."

Does she have amplified hearing as well as her powers?

"Yes, I was just wondering where he was," said Amelia. "I… he said I could talk to him if I needed anything."

Samantha eyed her silently. It made Amelia feel nervous and self aware. She felt the elevator doors slide open behind her and jumped a bit.

"Check the pool," said Samantha. "Second floor. That's where he spends most of his nights. Swimming helps him relax, apparently."

"Oh, right… Thanks," said Amelia.

She stepped into the elevator and breathed a sigh of relief as the doors slid shut. Why did she have to be so intimidating? It was difficult to give her a chance and feel relaxed when she had the constant feeling that Samantha was analysing her every move.

She made her way down to the second floor and approached the pool area that she had seen earlier. It was a wide room, enclosed completely in dark glass. The pool itself was 500 meters, with five different lanes. As she got closer she could hear a rhythmic splashing that confirmed Apollo was, in fact, there.

She slowly walked closer to the water's edge but kept her distance. Perhaps for obvious reasons, she had never been too keen on water. She watched as Apollo made his way from the opposite side of the pool and looked up towards her. There was a wide grin on his face when he noticed she was here.

"Hey! What brings you down here?" he called from the middle of the pool.

He made his way to her, and came to rest on the pool's edge, his chin resting on his arms.

"Care to join me for a swim?" he asked.

"Um, no thanks," she said.

"You sure? The water's great," he said. "It's nice and warm."

"I'm not really a great swimmer. Not too fond of water either."

"Well, who knew?" he said, laughing. "That's one thing you have in common with Sam! She absolutely hates water. She only learned how to swim in case of extreme emergencies, but she will never get in for entertainment. Maybe the two of you can bond over that one piece of interesting trivia."

"I don't think the two of us will be bonding over anything soon," said Amelia, her tone a bit discouraged.

"Was it that bad?" Apollo asked.

Amelia simply nodded. She felt tears forming in her eyes and breathed deeply to make them go away.

"Give me a minute," he said, as he jumped out of the pool.

He picked up a nearby towel, patted himself dry and then guided her to a couple of cozy lounge chairs in the far side of the pool room.

"She told me what she said to you," he said.

"So, you know the choices she gave me?"

He nodded and reached for her hand.

"Listen, Ames, I know that you feel she's very harsh," he said.

"You think she's not?"

"I think there is too much going through her mind," he said. "But, I don't think she's being fair with you. I'm going to have a talk to her tomorrow. Try to get her to tone it down a bit. I know she doesn't want you to leave. She just gave you that ultimatum, so you would choose to stay and train."

"Can you get her to tone it down a lot?" Amelia asked.

"I will definitely try," he said, with a smile.

Once again, as she spoke to Apollo she could not help but feel calm. There was something about him, in his demeanour, that made things seem alright, at least for a while. He emanated kindness. These two people were certainly opposites. Samantha was tough and firm, Apollo kind and gentle. How these two managed to coexist and not kill each other was beyond Amelia's understanding.

"Have you given any thought to your training?" Apollo asked.

"Yes… I know that I should continue," said Amelia. "It's the logical thing to do. But, sometimes it's not easy to do what's logical… I'm scared, to be perfectly honest."

"Maybe, it could help if you tell me why you're so scared," said Apollo. "Sometimes, things aren't as bad when you say them out loud. Or when you share the burden with someone else."

She considered this for a moment. She thought about the last time she had had someone to talk to – to really talk to – about her problems and fears. It had been almost three years now, since she had lost the closest person to her. She tried to block out that memory, which brought nothing but heartache and pain.

"I wouldn't even know where to begin," she said, shyly. "So many things have happened."

He adjusted his glasses and looked at her, giving her his full attention.

"Just start anywhere," he said. "Anything you tell me can stay between us, if that's what you would like. I promise not to judge you. I'm here for whatever you need."

Amelia took a few seconds and breathed in deeply. Without wanting to give it much further thought, she started talking.

"As long as I can remember, I've been afraid of my powers," she said. "That much I think I've made clear. There are so many things about my past that are a blur, that I don't remember very clearly, but, I think the first memories that I have that make sense are from when I arrived at Saint Agne's Orphanage."

"You grew up in an orphanage?" Apollo asked, his tone somber. "I would have never thought... How did you end up there?"

"Well, I was so young, wandering the streets on my own," she said. "One day, a woman took me in. She said she knew the orphanage's director and that they would be able to help me find a home. I know she meant well, but my time in that place was anything but peaceful."

"What do you mean?"

"The other kids there, they thought I was different," she said. "I didn't really bond with anyone. I was afraid that if I got close to anyone I could hurt them. So, the others made fun of me, for being a loner, they picked on me, made life a living hell. Even the adults thought I was different. On one occasion, I was by myself in the room and I started a small fire... It was an accident, I called for help and a couple of the teachers came and put it out. They were so confused as to how I was able to start a fire. They were afraid of me after that, thought I was some sort of dangerous pyromaniac."

Apollo smirked. "Well, you technically are."

"Thanks," she said, smiling back. "That's really helpful. Anyway, after that, I tried as hard as I could to be more careful, but it didn't work. I caused a major fire one day, an entire wing of the orphanage burnt down. It was a miracle that no one was hurt. That was the day I decided to run away from there. I would not risk hurting anyone."

"Ames, I get why you're afraid," he said. "I really do. You're afraid you'll hurt people with your abilities. But, think about it, if you finally learn to control them, you can make sure you won't ever hurt anyone else again."

She did not answer. She knew he was right, of course, but that did not stop her from being afraid. It was not that easy, to change something that had been her nature for so long.

"It's getting really late," said Apollo. "How about we turn in and get some much needed rest. You might feel differently in the morning."

"I don't think many things will have changed from now until then," said Amelia. "I'll still be in a panic at the thought of Samantha training me."

"Well, of course," said Apollo, laughing. "That's one thing that will probably never go away."

He stood up and reached out his hand for her to follow him.

"Thanks for confiding a bit of your story in me," he said. "Hopefully, you will tell me more some other time."

"No problem," she said. "Thanks for listening… It feels good to have someone to rely on."

CHAPTER TEN

Choices can sometimes be a daunting thing. Most times, people want to take the easy way out, but the easy way is not usually the right way. It is scary to think of the consequences of making the wrong decision, doubts begin to creep in and things feel too much to handle, but the truth of the matter is, if risks are not taken there won't ever be a win.

The choices Amelia had been given were both difficult and she could not see the benefit to either of them. She did not want to train and use her abilities. She wanted so badly to not even have them. On the other hand, she definitely did not want to leave this place and be on her own again. She knew what she had to do but overcoming her fears would not be an easy thing.

She would continue with the training sessions, however dreadful they might be for her, and perhaps after more failed attempts Samantha would leave her alone – or kick her out of the house, taking away any chance she could have of a family.

After her chat with Apollo by the pool, she had come to her room, taken a quick shower and now lay in bed, trying to clear her mind. After a few minutes she dozed off, realizing how tired she was. Images began to flash through her mind. A fire, intense and destructive, surrounded her. She was inside a small house and the flames were consuming everything. She tried to stop it, but it only became stronger and stronger. She called out a name, yelled it out as loud as she could, but there was no answer.

The flames didn't hurt her, she could easily walk through them. She ran through the small house as the structure began to collapse around her. She checked room after room, he wasn't in any of them. She reached the small kitchen, once cozy and welcoming, now covered in bright flames and ashes, the wallpaper burnt away. Everything around her destroyed, because of her.

On the floor, in the middle of the flames, lay the man she had frantically searched for. She yelled out his name again, "DAVID!" Running through the flames she reached him and checked for a pulse. There was none. Tears began running down her face, leaving a trail down her cheeks, which were covered in ash and soot.

She took a hold of his arm and tried to pull his limp body out of the kitchen. No matter how hard she tried he would not budge. Time was running out; the flames had consumed too much of the house's structure and it was all coming down around her. She let go of his arm and whispered "I'm so sorry... I'm sorry..."

She ran outside where the fresh air made it easier to breathe. She stood and watched the flames become fiercer, wilder. The house was no longer visible. She heard sirens at a distance and knew that she had to run. If she was caught, there was no telling what would happen to her.

"Ames? Ames, wake up!"

She awoke startled and disoriented. She looked around and realized it had all been a dream. Apollo sat beside her, his hand on her shoulder, his face had a look of deep concern.

"Are you okay?" he asked, his voice gentle, soothing.

She felt her face and noticed that tears had been streaming down as she dreamed.

"Who is David?" he asked.

She hesitated, feeling uncomfortable. She must have been yelling out in her sleep, that's why he was here. "No one." She answered simply.

He looked at her but did not push for an answer. She was grateful for this.

"You know that if you ever want to talk about it, I'm here for you," he said.

"Thanks… I'm sorry… I feel like I'm causing you guys too much trouble."

"You're not. You are a part of this very dysfunctional family unit we have. We spent so many years trying to find you, it's a relief to have you back home."

Home, family. She was not used to hearing these words when relating to herself. Fear, loneliness, darkness. Those were the words that defined her life. Apollo got up to leave but she called him back.

"Polo, wait… About what Sam spoke to me earlier…"

He nodded.

"I've decided to train again."

"That's good to hear… Was there anything else on your mind?"

She didn't answer straight away, instead she looked intently down at her hands, as if there was something written on them that could explain what she was feeling.

"I'm still afraid – I know what my powers can do… I've seen it… I'm afraid of hurting you and not being able to control it."

"I know you are," he said. "I also believe that you can beat your fear. You can push past it. Don't allow it to control you any longer. If you do, it will take over... There will be no turning back if you let it consume you. We are here to help, to guide you through something that we have already been through. You just need to have a bit of faith and let us in."

****

Michael opened his eyes slowly. There was a bright light above him, making it hard to see his surroundings. He knew where he was, though. He had been here many times before. This was the room where he had been experimented on.

He was strapped to a cold examination table, both arms and legs restrained with thick leather bindings, unable to move even an inch. Snyde had learned from previous mistakes. One time, during one of these sessions Michael had broken free and given his men a good run for their money. He smiled at the memory.

He turned his head to one side, trying to see if anyone was in the room with him. As soon as he moved he felt his head swirl. The drugs they were using to sedate him were getting stronger. He blinked a few times, hoping this would help.

"Please stay still," said a woman's cold voice from his left.

That answered his question, he was not alone.

"What does he want now?" asked Michael, his voice was slurred.

"That's nothing you need to worry about." She walked over to the table and connected an IV line into both his arms. "This might hurt, so worry about that."

As soon as she had spoken these words, Michael felt as his insides began to burn. He screamed, the pain was excruciating. He had never felt anything quite like this. His blood felt like it was on fire, his entire body was burning from the inside. He struggled against his restraints, writhing in pain. He needed this to stop, he could not take much more of this.

****

"Ready for another round?" asked Samantha as they walked into the large training hangar the following morning.

"I guess so," Amelia replied rather unconvincingly.

"Just remember, we're here to help you," said Apollo. "There is no need to be scared."

Samantha guided Amelia to the middle of the room, Apollo taking a seat behind the room's control board. Today, the room appeared to be empty. Amelia looked around, up at the ceiling, at the floor, but still could not spot what the target for her training would be today.

"So, today we're going to do something a bit different," said Samantha. "I am going to practice with you. I'll talk you through the exercises and we can practice them together."

At hearing this, Amelia became even more stressed. It was no secret by now that Samantha intimidated her, so this was not exactly the calming news she had been hoping for.

"Are you... sure this is a... good idea?" she mumbled the words.

"Leaving you on your own clearly was not going to work, so this seems like the next best thing."

To Amelia, this felt like someone had simply told her 'since you were not able to learn to swim in a pool, we'll throw you into a lava pit inhabited by fire breathing dragons'. Not necessarily what she had been hoping for, but there was no turning back now, or she was sure to feel the wrath of this particular dragon.

"Let's begin. Apollo will monitor us and if anything gets out of hand he can control it with his powers, so you have nothing to worry about."

Amelia nodded her head and took a deep breath. Her hands were sweaty, and she was sure that Samantha would be able to hear her heart beat, as it was racing a million miles per second.

"The first thing I want you to do is ignite a simple fireball and hold it in the palm of your hand."

"I'm not sure I know how to," Amelia admitted.

"You have to start by clearing your mind," said Samantha. "Clear it of any doubts or fears you might have. Then, you must feel the energy coursing through your veins… Don't think about it, just feel it. The fire is a natural part of you. It flows through you, inside you – you control it, not the other way around."

Amelia closed her eyes. She tried to focus all her attention into creating a small flame. During the first few attempts nothing happened, she pictured the fire in her mind, but her body would not match that image. She opened and closed her hand several times, not really thinking this would help much, but simply to try something different. She could feel Samantha standing beside her, losing her patience.

She pictured the fire again and this time forced her body to go long with her mind. Fire burst to life in the palm of her hand.

"That's it!" said Samantha, enthusiastically. "Try to hold on to it."

Sweat dripped from Amelia's forehead, the effort of holding the flame was too overwhelming. The fire started to spread down her arm and onto the walls around them.

"Sam, I can't hold it!" her voice was filled with panic.

"Yes, you can!" Samantha retorted. "You *can* do it, just concentrate."

Even as she heard these words, Amelia began to lose what little control she had managed. The flames quickly began to spread out of hand, surrounding them both. Apollo quickly set up a force field around Samantha, to avoid her getting hurt.

"Amelia, it's okay, focus on my voice," said Apollo, his tone was soothing. "Don't worry about the fire, it won't hurt us. Focus on me."

Amelia took a few deep breaths and the flames began to subside. She ran over to Apollo and collapsed into his arms. He held her tightly, trying to calm her, she was shaking all over.

"You nearly had it! What happened?" asked Samantha, she sounded exasperated. "You have to try harder."

"I was trying as hard as I possibly could!" Amelia yelled.

"I don't believe you."

"I don't care what you believe!" Amelia shot back. "I'm not here to impress you."

"No, you're here to learn how to not die," said Samantha. "When they come for us and finally find us, you have to know how to fight back, if you don't then you will not survive, believe me."

"That's enough," Apollo intervened. "We are not getting anywhere with this continuous arguing."

"You're right... Amelia, take a few minutes to pull yourself together and then we'll try again."

"But –"

"Not buts, just go and come back in a few minutes."

Amelia leered at her and left the room huffing and mumbling under her breath. Once she had left, Apollo turned to Samantha, she was angry, even more than what he considered to be her normal.

"Do you want to tell me why you are being so hard on her?"

"I don't know what you mean," she said, her arms tightly crossed.

"Don't treat me like I can't read you better than anyone."

She sighed, knowing he was right. There was no way she could ever fool him, he knew her too well, perhaps even better than she did at times.

"I'm just so frustrated... She's holding back, there is something she's not telling us, and it could end up hurting all of us."

"She's been through a lot, Sam. You have to be more patient, she isn't used to her powers like we are. I think something happened to her, because of her abilities. Something she can't just get over as quickly as you would like."

"We need her to be ready... I won't be able to protect her forever."

"I don't think it's fair for you to take on that role. I've told you before, you don't have to be our protector."

"Yes, I do."

Apollo walked over to her and put his arms around her. She relaxed into his embrace. There was such strength in him, always giving her the support she needed. No matter how hard things got, he was always there for her.

"Bring her back for another try," said Samantha. "Let's see what we can do."

CHAPTER ELEVEN

The room was dark, the only faint source of light came from the slit at the bottom of the door. Michael tried to adjust his eyes to his new surroundings, but he was having a difficult time focusing. They had done something to him, the last experiment had left him feeling strange, like his mind was not all there and his body did not seem to respond like it always did. He clumsily felt around the floor, not looking for anything in particular.

His muscles ached, his mouth was dry, and his head felt like someone was pressing his brain against his skull. Before he could get accustomed to his new environment a violent bright light shone straight on him, like a spotlight. He blinked and tried to make out where the light was coming from. When his sight had adjusted he saw where he was. A large room, similar in shape to a roman fighting arena, several gates were spread across the room and a wide window stood high above.

From the window he could make out a dark figure looking down on him, the now familiar wicked smile on his face. Oleander Snyde was watching him with rapt attention.

"Mr. Clarke, how grand of you to finally awake," his voice was magnified, Michael's head pounded. "Now we can begin."

"What do you want from me?" asked Michael, weakly.

"You will see soon enough. I have brought you here to test my newest creation. The most magnificent creature, my greatest achievement to date – and the one thing that will finally help me find and capture your friends."

Snyde's smile widened as Michael looked on. Michael knew there was nothing that brought Snyde him more joy than causing pain. True and sincere pain, that was his main objective. Destruction, at massive scales.

"I have injected you with a new serum, making your immune system slow down temporarily. Your body will not be able to heal as quickly and you will feel your movements fail. I have done this for – shall we say, *entertainment* purposes only." His dark eyes shone with pleasure. "Now, release him."

One of the gates on the far side of the arena began to open. Michael tried as hard as he could to hold strong, the effects of the serum still in his system. It was painful to simply stand, he was not sure what was in store, but he was certain there was no way to come out of this situation unscathed. He considered himself to be brash and brave, but at this moment, only fear reigned inside him... for himself and the others. If it was true that whatever was behind this door could find them, he had to stop it.

****

The days began to turn into weeks and the weeks to months. Still, Amelia's progress was nowhere near what they had hoped. Every time she seemed to be gaining more confidence, something happened and she took two steps back.

Samantha's frustration was growing with each passing day, making training sessions increasingly difficult.

"Try again!" she said, harsher than she had intended.

Amelia looked exhausted, she had been practicing for the last four hours, trying as hard as she could to create and control a ring of fire around different targets set across the room. Half of the targets had been completely incinerated by now and the surviving targets were headed in the same direction. No matter how hard she tried, she was never able to stop the fire. It would spread wildly, taking Apollo at least ten minutes at a time to put out and set up new targets around the room.

"This isn't easy for me!" said Amelia, her own frustration rising.

"You're not giving it your all! You are still holding back, after all these weeks and everything we've talked about… I don't know what else you want from us." Samantha walked out of the room, leaving Amelia and Apollo behind to clean up the latest blaze's victims.

"What does she want from me?"

"I know she isn't the most tactful person, she just… well, she thought that you might have improved a bit more… with so much practice, that's all."

Amelia gave him a killer look. "You agree with her, I suppose."

He raised his hands, not wanting to start a fight. "Hey, I'm on your side, remember?"

"I know… I'm sorry, Polo. I just – I know you don't believe me, but I wish I was better. I don't want to be this useless person, causing you guys more grief and pain, being a danger to everyone."

"I believe you want to improve, but you can't do that until you truly let go of what holds you back."

"What do you mean?"

"Your nightmares, you still have them every night."

Amelia looked embarrassed. "I'm not sure what you're talking about."

"Yes, you do. My room is next to yours, remember? I can hear you, screaming. Most nights you just yell out nonsense, other nights you call out his name, over and over. David. You still won't tell me who he is."

He knew she did not like this topic. Every time it came up, she tried to change the subject or simply walked away from it. He had not mentioned her nightmares to Samantha. Amelia had asked him not to, this was not something she wanted brought out, so he had agreed but, perhaps the moment had come when she needed to get past what haunted her sleep every night.

"How would you like to go somewhere else for a while? We can get out of the house, get some fresh air, have a coffee."

"Are we even allowed to?"

"Come on, Ames, this isn't a prison, you know that. This is your home now."

"Sometimes it feels like it," Amelia admitted.

"And Sam is the warden?"

Amelia burst out laughing. The moments of joy in her life had been so few and often short lived, so she had learned to appreciate each one.

"I don't think Sam would object to us getting a bite and a drink, *but* perhaps it would be safer if we don't mention it, lets just make a run for it. It's better to ask for forgiveness than for permission, I think."

"She is going to be furious," said Amelia, trying hard to hide her smile.

"Nah, just leave her to me," said Apollo. "She'll be fine."

Apollo drove the truck up the lonely road leading out of The Bunker. They would head to the closest town, an hour and a half away. The day was sunny and warm, and Amelia had her window down, enjoying the wind that blew softly against her face and through her hair. She could not remember the last time she had fully paid attention to these simple things. It had only been a few months since she had been alone and scared, not sure what her next move would be and where her next meal would come from.

Things had changed a lot for her in a very short time so, she could not help but wonder how long this could last. Her life had not been a happy one, she was afraid that if she started to feel happiness, safety, things that other people took for granted, that it would all be taken from her.

After half an hour they pulled up at a small restaurant. It was almost five in the afternoon, so the place was not very busy, only a few people were in for an early dinner. They took a table near the back and were quickly served by a young girl whose name tag read 'Adler' and who only had eyes for Apollo. She flirted blatantly with him, giggling at his every comment. Amelia rolled her eyes at their exchange, focusing on her water glass rather than on their conversation.

Once they had placed their order and the girl had walked off, Amelia turned her attention towards the window, watching cars driving past. Her mind wandered off, she was not thinking about anything in particular, just taking the moment in.

"Are you okay?

Amelia nodded. "I'm just a bit tired. This is all very draining for me, I'm not used to actually trying to use my powers. I've spent most of my life trying to hide them."

"I understand, I truly do. But, Ames, you have to understand something as well. We want to help you, so that you can be comfortable with the person that you are. It's not easy being different, but it's even harder if you don't let other people in. Sam and I, we've both been through the same things you are going through, even if it has been at a different level."

"I want to let you in, Polo. But –"

"What? Tell me what you are so afraid of?"

"If I tell you, I might push you away. I will end up on the losing end, like I always do."

"Take my word for it, you can't lose us. We are in this thing together, whether you like it or not. We will stick together, no matter what happens. Even Sam. Trust me."

Amelia considered his words, she knew she could trust him, he was the closest friend she had had in such a long time, he was starting to feel like she thought a brother would. She took a deep breath and began to speak. "You want to know who David is?"

Apollo nodded but didn't interrupt her.

"I might as well start at the very beginning, or with the pieces I remember at least. After the night when we were all separated, I waited for Finn to come back for me, but he never did. For a few days I stayed in the deserted apartment where I had hidden, too scared to leave in case he really did come for me. When I realized he was not coming back, I left the apartment in search of food. I was just a little girl, alone in the streets, begging for food, scavenging through garbage bins."

Apollo listened intently to her story, knowing how hard this was for her to share.

"I caught people's attention," she said. "The woman I told you about took me to the orphanage. During my time there, I was sent to a couple of families, but they always sent me back. I was too much to handle, something would always happen."

The waitress interrupted by bringing their meals. Amelia looked up at her and thanked her, but she just had smiles for Apollo. She turned her attention back to her story.

"Anyway, fires started, people were afraid. I was afraid. After the last time I was sent back, you know what happened... I caused the fire that burnt down half the orphanage. It was a miracle that no one was hurt... I ran. I was fourteen at the time... Alone on the streets again, I met David. He approached me, asked me what I was doing all alone. Where my family was... There was something about him, I felt like I could trust him. He was so kind and so welcoming... You remind me of him a bit."

Apollo smiled at her. Still he said nothing, he was completely drawn into her story. He felt sorry for all the hard times she had been through. No matter how bad they had felt, they had always had each other for comfort and they had always had all the food and supplies they had needed.

"He took me in, offered me a place to stay, warm food, he offered me a home. After a couple of months living with him I decided to trust David with my secret, I told him about my powers. He wasn't scared, he didn't kick me out, on the other hand, he tried to protect me. He told me that I had to be extra careful and never let anyone else know about them, that people wouldn't understand, that they would try to hurt me. I think my fear grew with every passing day.

I felt my powers, I don't know exactly how to describe it, but they wanted to come out, no matter how much I tried to keep them hidden. One night, they were too strong for me to hold back and I started a fire... It was so powerful, so deadly... I wasn't – I –"

She was holding back tears. The memory of what happened next was too hard for her to go on. Apollo reached out and held her hands. "It's okay, Ames, you don't have to go into this if you don't want to."

She took a deep breath and dried her tears with the back of her hand. "I need to, I've never told anyone this... I want to tell you. The fire spread all through the house. I tried to find David, to get him to safety. I searched everywhere, the fire was consuming everything around the house, the walls, the furniture. It was like walking through hell, everywhere you looked there was fire. It didn't harm me, but I knew that no one else could possibly survive something like that. I found him, he was unconscious, laying on the kitchen floor. I tried dragging him out, but he was too heavy for me. The house began to collapse and I – I had to –"

"You had to leave him, if you hadn't, you would both be dead." Apollo finished gently. "It wasn't you fault, there was nothing else you could have done for him."

"It *was* my fault, if I didn't have these powers – or if I could at least control them, David would still be alive... I should have done more... Tried harder."

"I know you think that way, but at the time, there was nothing more you could do. Even though we have all these abilities, we aren't immortal. You could have died if you had stayed in that house any longer. It would have collapsed on you."

Amelia nodded, but was still not too convinced of what he was saying.

"Why hadn't you told me this before?" Apollo asked.

"I guess – I was – I thought that you wouldn't want me around, after knowing that because of me, someone was dead."

"I would have never thought that," he said. "It was an accident. You didn't want any of it to happen."

Amelia did not answer. She dried more tears from her eyes.

"Look, it was logical to be afraid of your abilities, you never got to see a positive side to them."

"Fire only causes destruction," said Amelia, bitterly, she looked down at her hands as if they were dirty, tainted somehow.

"This fire is a part of who you are. You have to accept it. Embrace it. Feel comfortable with who you are. That feeling you describe, how it wanted to come out, I feel it every day. We all do, but we embrace it. I know how amazing my abilities can be and all the good I can do by learning how to harness them correctly."

"No offense, Polo, I just can't see how your powers could destroy others."

"Look at it this way, I have the ability to control all the air around me, and that doesn't mean just the external air in the environment. I told you once before, I can control the air inside people, I could easily take a life if I didn't know how to control it – but on the other hand, I can give someone a breath of life if they ever need it. Your fire, it very easily has the capability to destroy, but you could also use it to help, to bring light to darkness. It all has to do with perspective. I know you never intentionally meant to hurt anyone, David saw the good in you, he wasn't afraid of what you could do… I am not afraid of what you can do. *You* just need to stop being afraid of what you can do."

At that point in the conversation the waitress returned to check on their progress and offer refills for their drinks. She gave Apollo a wide grin and set down a small piece of paper next to his plate.

"Let me know if there is anything else I can do for you," she said, a bit more enthusiastically than was actually called for, and walked away.

"What's that?" Amelia pointed to the small piece of paper.

Apollo opened it and blushed slightly. "It's her phone number." He handed the piece of paper to Amelia who smirked.

"*Call me if you want to catch dinner sometime*." Amelia started to laugh. "Not the most inspiring phrase. I'm sure she could have thought of something more original."

"That's funny, although... I wouldn't really be interested either way."

"I really didn't think you would be," said Amelia, looking down at her meal. "You seem to be more drawn to the aggressive type."

"What's that supposed to mean?"

Amelia chuckled and almost choked on her last bite. "Please, Polo, I may be clueless about a lot of things, but I've seen the way you look at Sam."

"I swear I don't know what you mean." Apollo became suddenly fascinated by his own meal.

"Fine, be that way, I've just trusted you with my deepest secret and you can't even admit this one tiny thing."

"Well, look I guess... I guess I don't find Sam *unattractive* —"

"You're joking?" Amelia asked. "*Unattractive?* You *do* realize she's gorgeous, don't you?"

"That's really... I mean, that's beside the point," he stammered. "Anyway, she has more important things to worry about than what I might think about her."

"Hmm, you are right, she probably has no time for silly things like feelings," Amelia added playfully.

"Sam's not as bad as you think. She just has a lot on her plate. The two of you just need to cut each other some slack."

"Hey, lecture *her* about it," said Amelia. "Speaking of Sam, she's going to kill us, isn't she?"

"She will at least try. But, don't worry about it. I'll talk to her, this was all my idea, so you shouldn't have to take the blame for it. I'll sort it out."

CHAPTER TWELVE

Lunch had been a great idea. Amelia felt as if some of the weight had been lifted off her shoulders. She even felt like she was ready to give training another chance. As they pulled up to The Bunker, some of those elated feelings began to escape. She was dreading facing Samantha, who was bound to be beyond furious. Perhaps she would finally kick her out on the street, leaving her to fend for herself again.

They drove past the strong waterfall covering the entrance and waited as the truck was lowered onto the underground parking. Amelia thought about telling him to turn back and they could simply run away, but he continued forward and parked the truck. Apollo could sense her nervousness and gave her a huge smile.

"Don't be silly, nothing bad is going to happen."

"Let's just get this over with."

They got out of the car and walked inside. Everything was dark in the entrance hall, the kitchen and the living room.

"You see, she's gone to bed, nothing to worry about."

He had barely finished his sentence when the lights came on in the living room. Samantha was sitting on the black leather couch, her expression hard to read. She was not displaying any emotion. Amelia took one glance at her and could not decide if this meant she was angry, belligerent, or just plain murderous.

"Sam, I –" Amelia began to speak but Samantha cut her off.

"Give us a moment, please, Amelia? I want a word with Apollo."

She did not need to be asked twice. She mumbled a quick good night and headed straight for her room.

"Before you start, let me just say –"

Samantha cut him off as well.

"I need to understand what you were thinking," her tone was standoffish.

He wasn't able to read just how angry she was or what she was thinking, something he was usually pretty good at.

"Or maybe, you weren't thinking at all," she continued. "You are not a child anymore, Apollo, so I'm not going to treat you like one. You must have thought full well about the possible consequences of your actions."

"Sam, nothing bad was going to happen! We just went out for lunch."

"And you knew that nothing bad would happen? Even though you were going to lunch with the most unstable person when it comes to her abilities. Her powers are dangerous. You *know* this, she could have lost control at any moment, hurting not just you but everyone else around you."

"Nothing happened."

"You keep saying that, but it's really not the point! It's the fact that those thoughts didn't even cross your mind, did they? To you, it's all about the optimism, everything in your mind is happy and amazing all the time, but let me tell you, life is not always like that."

Samantha's tone was changing with every word, now he could easily tell how upset she was. But it wasn't just anger in her voice, there was something more, there was a hint of pain.

"Did you for one second stop to think about what would have happened if she had lost control and the police had been called? What could you have done if people had gotten hurt? Do you think that you could have kept her safe if the police had come for you? You could have been tracked down and taken. One false move, that's all it takes. Haven't you caught on to that by now? After all we have lived through. After all that Alex taught us, did it not even cross your mind to be more careful?"

Apollo felt ashamed, a guilty knot forming in his stomach. In all honesty, he had not stopped to think about any of these things. He just wanted to help Amelia loosen up, to get her in a more relaxed environment, so she could feel better.

"I have been sitting here for the past four hours wondering what I would do if you had been taken."

"Sam, I'm so sorry but nothing bad happened, we're both fine... it doesn't matter anymore," he walked closer to her and tried to hold her, but she backed away.

"No, it's not that simple," she said, running her hands through her hair. "You don't get to just hug me and fix things. Not this time. I am beyond furious with you. I would have thought that after all we've been through – after they took Mikey – that you would think about the consequences of your actions."

"I'm not Michael... I'm here with you, Sam."

"That's what he thought, that nothing would ever go wrong. Then, we got careless and he was gone... You think I'm the bad one, for worrying about you – about both of you, you make me out to be so tough and rough, well life can't all be fun and games. Not our life, at least. Just think about it – if I lose you, what that would do to me?"

"Sam, please don't be this way."

Samantha gave hime one final look and walked out of the room, leaving him feeling worse than he ever thought possible.

****

Snyde felt elated as he peered down on Michael's broken and nearly mangled figure, blood covered the floors and walls of the room. He was still alive, but only just and would heal fully in the next couple of days. Snyde was not ready to kill the boy, not yet. Soon he would no longer have any use for him, but for the time being he would keep him for further testing of his new serums and creations. He was the perfect guinea pig.

"Take him back to his cell," he said to the guard standing behind him.

"So, how was he?" A woman appeared by his side. Her voice cold, wicked and almost inhuman.

"The creature was better than I hoped," replied Snyde. "He is ready for the field and his first task will be to track down the others."

"Let me go with him, I can be of help. I want to bring them to you myself."

"No, you will stay here. I won't risk you getting hurt. He will go after them and bring them back to me."

"What if he fails?"

"He will not fail, not after what I have just witnessed."

****

"Again!" Samantha called out harshly.

Today's training had been nothing short of horrifying. Samantha's mood had not improved at all since the previous night and she was having no problem taking her frustration out on Amelia, who sat on the floor, exhausted and out of breath.

"Get up and try again."

Amelia did as she was told, arguing did not seem like the best option taking the current atmosphere into account. In the large training room there had been fifteen hanging dummies and her task was, once again, to create fire rings around them, without setting them ablaze. So far, thirteen had been burned to a crisp and the two that remained were almost certainly looking at the same fate.

Amelia took a few deep breaths and managed to ignite two large fireballs in her hands. Now for the tricky part, using that to surround the dummies without lighting them. She released one of the fireballs and it landed next to the nearest dummy, dancing around it for a few seconds before it was completely engulfed in flames.

"Forget it, I still don't have enough control," she said, disappointed at her lack of improvement. Even though she was so afraid of these powers, she really was trying as hard as she could to get better, for all their sakes.

"You're doing your best," Apollo added, encouragingly. "There's not much more we can ask for."

Samantha gave him one of the coldest looks she had ever seen. He put his hands up indicating he did not want another fight to erupt between them.

"Amelia, give us a moment," said Samantha, after a few minutes of silence.

She was more than glad to be out of this room, so she quickly complied. She had only walked a few paces when she heard yelling from inside the training room. Poor Apollo was not getting the easy end of her temper. Her plan had not been to eavesdrop, but she could not help it, Samantha was yelling so loudly.

"I've had ENOUGH!"

"Calm down, Sam. You know there's no need for this."

"HOW CAN YOU SAY THAT? It's been almost three months! And what do we have to show for it? I *have* tried, I've been as patient as I know how. But I can't do this anymore! She is not getting better, she will hurt herself or one of us! If she is not an asset to us, then she is a burden and you know this!"

"Sam! You don't mean that. She has gotten better, but maybe it's all too much pressure for her. She is only seventeen years old."

"That is no excuse! Look at yourself, you're only eighteen! I know you want to protect her, but there is no reason for her to not be improving at a much faster pace. I'm serious, if she doesn't get better and I mean soon, she's better off on her own."

"So, what? You would really kick her out?" Apollo asked.

"You know I wouldn't," she said softly.

A few tears were building up on Amelia's eyes. She quickly wiped them away and ran towards her room. She was exhausted, tired of being thought of as a burden, of putting others in danger because of her inability to control her powers.

She was determined to not put anyone else at risk. She would leave, that way Samantha would be happy, and they wouldn't have to worry about her every minute of the day. It was the best thing for everyone. She packed a small bag and snuck out before the others could realize she was gone. This was the best thing to do, no matter if it broke her heart to leave the only place where she had finally felt at home.

CHAPTER THIRTEEN

"What do you mean 'she's gone'?"

"I mean, I can't find her anywhere in the house. She's gone!" Apollo exclaimed.

Samantha cursed under her breath. "She must have heard what I said."

"Well, you were yelling like a deranged mental patient."

"This is not the time," she answered, rolling her eyes. "Come on, get your coat. She couldn't have gone too far, she's on foot. We'll take the truck."

"What if we don't find her?"

"That's not an option," answered Samantha. "I never should have been so hard on her... This is all my fault."

"Don't say that – even though it kind of is, but still."

"Just – come on, we're wasting time."

They ran out the door and jumped into the truck. She started the engine and stepped down on the gas, going as fast as she could. Amelia had to be close by, she probably only had around twenty minutes head start. The night was dark and freezing cold, it was hard to see anything, specially not a person walking on her own.

"Keep your eyes open," she said to Apollo.

Her voice betrayed her nerves and the anxiety she was feeling. How could she have let this get so out of hand? She had been thoughtless, careless and if anything happened to this helpless girl it was all on her.

****

She had been walking down the dark road for the past ten minutes, not knowing where to go or what her next move would be, just knowing that she had to get as far away as possible. She wiped the tears that ran down her face as she continued to walk. Her body was numb from the cold, shivering all over but she refused to use her powers, it was not safe here.

After a few more minutes she wondered off the main road and sat down under a large tree to rest. A wave of exhaustion took over, her body drained both physically and emotionally. It would be fine if she just closed her eyes for a few minutes, only to rest, she was not going to sleep, it would be dangerous.

She opened her eyes and found herself inside a small store. It looked like a local grocery. She scanned the small area and soon saw someone she recognized. It was Finn, he was standing at the checkout counter, watching as the man at the register scanned a few items. This was a weird dream. She appeared to be looking at the scene in the third person, but no one noticed she was in the room. No person in the dream acknowledge her being there. Then, she noticed the man stop while scanning one item. His gaze was fixed on something behind Finn.

Suddenly, there was a horrible scream from behind. Finn spun around and saw what had caused the commotion. Amelia followed Finn's line of sight and felt her pulse quicken. A few feet away she saw herself, at a much younger age. Her seven year old self was standing a few feet from them, her hands alight with bright flames, the counter in front of her ablaze. She looked around for Finn, her face showed all the fear that was going through her.

Bright orange flames were quickly spreading throughout the small store. The man behind the counter ran towards young Amelia, yelling at her as he approached. "What did you do?!"

Finn stepped in front of him before he could reach her.

"Leave her alone," he said forcefully. "She's just a child, it was an accident!"

"She is not a child! And that was no accident!" the man said. "I saw it with my own eyes! She caused it… she… she made the fire start! Out of thin air… she's a monster! A freak! I'm calling the police!"

Finn grabbed the man's arm, "You can't! You don't understand, she didn't mean any harm."

"Let go of me! How do I know you're not a freak of nature, just like her? I'm calling the cops!"

The fire continued to spread as the two men argued. The other customers ran from the store as the smoke filled the small space. Amelia looked on in horror as she saw her seven year old self sitting on the floor, hugging her legs tight to her body. Her hands were still on fire and she cried out for Finn.

He ran over and tried to calm her. If she could remain calm, she would be able to control the fire. The store clerk had disappeared, probably calling the police at this very moment.

Once the police got word of this, Snyde would surely know. His people were infiltrated inside all the major law enforcement offices.

"Amelia, I need you to breathe." He got as close to her as he could without getting burned.

She didn't look up at him but continued crying. The fire around them was spreading too quickly, it was out of control. Sirens could be heard in the distance. The police and fire department were on their way.

Amelia was still sobbing uncontrollably, and her hands and chest were covered in bright flames. The sound from the sirens was getting louder and louder as each second passed.

"Amelia, honey, I need you to listen to me," whispered Finn, keeping the urgency and fear out of his voice. "We need to get out of here, it's dangerous. You have to calm down, I know it's hard for you to control, but I need you to try."

Her sobs subsided a little. He continued to speak. "You're not in any trouble, but we have to go – fast. Now, try as hard as you can to make the flames stop. Please, just close your eyes and breathe."

She looked up at him, her tiny eyes filled with tears, her expression somber. She breathed in and out slowly a few times. At first, nothing happened, but after a few more seconds passed, the flames around her began to extinguish.

"That's it! Good girl, just a bit more." Finn looked around. The whole place was full of smoke, the fire had spread too quickly. They would have to find a back exit, away from the patrol cars arriving just at the front. Amelia could see the red and blue lights reflecting on the walls around them.

After just a few more seconds the flames that surrounded Amelia's body had completely vanished and Finn picked her up, holding her close to him, making sure she remained calm in amidst of all this chaos. He walked rapidly but carefully through the thick smoke, coughing as he went. They needed to get out before it was too late. Struggling, he managed to make his way to the back of the store and spotted the exit.

In her dream, Amelia followed Finn and her younger self as he pushed open the door and exited the grocery store. He began walking as fast as he could down the street without drawing attention to them.

He still held Amelia in his arms, trying to shield her from view as much as possible.

"We have to hurry," said Finn. "We have to get to Alex and the others. We have to leave tonight; the police will come for us. It's not safe anymore."

From this scene, everything became blurry. Amelia watched on as the scenery in her dream changed. She saw Finn fade away and then, suddenly found herself on a building rooftop, rain drops falling heavily all around. She heard voices, but they were very muffled, and she could not make out what they were saying. She walked towards the sounds. After a few paces she saw Finn again. He was on his knees, three men pointed guns at him.

She tried to call out to him, to help him, but no sound came out. It was like she was immersed in a movie, watching it from the inside but not having any effect on the outcome. A woman approached, she could not see her face but only heard her sinister voice. She walked closer to the scene, curious about this woman, something drawing her nearer.

As she approached she heard a loud bang, a gunshot. When she looked around for the source she found herself back under the tree where she had fallen fast asleep. Something moved. She quickly got to her feet, scoping her surroundings, trying to detect the source of the movement.

"Hello? Is someone there?"

There was no answer. She felt wide awake now. Panic – real panic – was setting in. Her hear drummed against her ribs. She tried to calm herself and think it was probably nothing to be worried about, a wild animal or a stray dog. She picked up her bag and decided it was time to keep moving. She ran towards the main road again but found her path blocked by a massive dark figure.

It was unlike anything she had ever seen before. It had the look of a man but that was an impossibility, it towered over her. She froze, too scared to make any sudden movement. The creature started forward, quicker than she had expected due to its size. She tried to back away, but the creature was too agile. It swung out a massive arm and knocked her back. She crawled around the ground, dazed and confused.

The creature was leaning over her, she gasped as she took in it features. Where any normal person would have a face there was nothing, just darkness. It reached over and grabbed her, picking her up by her neck. She couldn't breath. She tried to kick out at the creature, but it was no use, she could feel herself losing consciousness with every passing second. Its grip was too tight, there was no way to get air into her lungs. The last thing she recalled was looking at the creature's black empty face and then nothingness.

****

The creature dropped her down to the ground hard, it grasped the scruff of her shirt and began dragging her away. It had found one of its intended targets, now it would return it to its master and begin searching for the others. It could sense they were not far away. It sniffed the air, definitely there were others like her nearby. It had been created with the ability to detect variations in their DNA.

It was time to return, it would take at least three days walk to go back to the lab. It would have to be careful to not be detected, the Master did not want to draw any attention. The creature continued to walk slowly, dragging the girl's limp form behind it.

****

Samantha slammed her foot down on the breaks, making the truck come to an abrupt stop. Standing in the middle of the road was a massive dark figure. It was human in form, but there was little else that looked human about it. It stood at almost 7 feet, with skin resembling black rubber and a face that was not a face at all. There were no eyes, no mouth, no nose. It stood there, blocking the road. In its gruesome hands it held a limp figure. Amelia. She dangled off his grip like a marionette.

"What in the world is that thing?" asked Apollo, in shock. "It has her, what do we do now?"

Samantha just stared at the creature in front of them, too many questions whirling around her mind, not knowing what to do or what its weakness might be – if it even had one – but knowing that they had to get Amelia back. They couldn't let it take her.

"You stay here," said Samantha. Apollo was about to argue, but she spoke again. "I mean it, Polo, no matter what happens you have to stay here. I can handle this myself."

"Are you insane? Are you not seeing the same thing I am? Because, no offense, but you *cannot* handle that thing! I'm not letting you face it on your own!"

"Yes, you are. I won't be able to focus if I have to worry about you getting hurt on top of everything else."

Apollo did not look convinced. This creature – whatever it was – was not likely to go down easily.

"Don't worry about me, I'll be fine. We have to get Amelia back."

Without another word, she opened the door and stepped out of the truck. Samantha walked slowly towards the immense dark figure. It didn't even seem to notice that she was coming closer. It turned around and continued to drag Amelia beside him.

Samantha hastened her step. The creature seemed to walk in slow motion, but its steps were so wide that it advanced at a much faster pace. Samantha was almost running now to try and keep up. When she was at a much closer distance to it, she charged her hands with as much electricity as she could and released it towards the creature. It stopped in its tracks, but the electricity that hit its body hadn't done a single thing to hurt it. It appeared to not even have fully processed what had just happened. It reacted as though a pesky fly had bumped against it and flown on.

The creature turned slowly and simply stood there. There was no expression on its dark, blank face, so Samantha couldn't make out whether the creature could see her or even know she was there. The creature let out a loud roar-like sound. It was so strong Samantha covered her ears. Before she had time to react, it released Amelia from its grasp and ran directly towards Samantha.

She had not been expecting such speed. She managed to jump out of the way right on time. She attacked the creature with another jolt of energy. All the electricity appeared to be absorbed by its armoured body.

This was clearly not going to be easy. The creature turned back towards Samantha and stood very still for a moment. Then, it seemed to be sucking in as much air as he could, even though there was no mouth, it seemed to be breathing in. Then, from its hands came a burst an intense energy, striking the ground next to where Samantha stood, spraying dirt and debris all over her.

What was this thing? It was unlike anything they had faced before or anything that Snyde had sent after them.

Just keep calm, Samantha thought to herself. Like all things, this creature must have strengths and weaknesses, the latter not being as apparent as the first. There had to be something it was vulnerable to. She tried sending bolt after bolt of electricity towards it, one after the other, each stronger than the last. Nothing. Each bolt disappeared into nothingness. She was exhausted, but she had to keep trying.

The creature turned on her once more, sending another energy beam her way. This time, the beam caught her off guard and struck her shoulder. The most awful pain she had ever felt pierced her entire body. She fell to her knees, yelling in pain. She looked at her shoulder. The place where the beam had hit had burned through her coat and the skin beneath it looked red and raw. It made her whole body burn.

Her vision blurred, she tried to think past the pain. Tried to focus on where the creature was. It stood a few feet away, but it was running towards her fast. She struggled to her feet, forcing the pain away. She would heal, everything would be fine, if she could only find a way to hurt it.

Her electric charges weren't doing anything to harm the creature, she had to try physical attacks. *Am I strong enough?* Samantha looked around for anything she could use as a weapon. Nothing. She would just have to use her own strength. She took a deep breath and ran towards the creature. She aimed a perfectly timed kick towards the creature's left side and struck. The creature didn't flinch. She tried once more. Nothing. Kick after kick, punch after punch and the creature just kept coming at her and throwing its own punches. She avoided the attacks as best she could, but after a few attempts, the creature landed a hit.

Samantha fell back, too winded and in too much agony to move. The creature reached her and picked her up by her neck. It was pain like she had never felt. She couldn't take any more of this. Hundreds of thoughts went through her head at that moment, as the creature squeezed the life out of her. Michael, she would never get to see him again and apologise for letting him down. Amelia, she regretted not being able to help her, to teach her how to control her abilities… and Apollo, her heart broke at the thought of leaving him alone, not being able to see his honest smile again. She had failed them all - failed Finn and Alexa and had not been able to keep her promise that she would protect them.

The creature, even with no face, somehow looked glad. It was fulfilling its main purpose. It would kill her and take Amelia back. She was losing consciousness fast, no matter how much she wanted to hold on, she just couldn't. At that moment, when everything seemed lost, the creature loosened its grip and released her, stumbling back a few steps.

She tried to see what had happened. Mustering every last bit of strength, she opened her eyes to see Apollo standing there.

"No…" she whispered.

Her voice was croaky and harsh. She didn't have enough strength to get back up. All she could do was watch in fear as the creature turned its full attention towards Apollo.

He stood his ground firmly, unflinching. He raised his hands towards the creature and Samantha felt rather than saw a strong gust of wind hit it. It stumbled slightly, but it didn't seem hurt. The creature stopped walking and once again released a beam of energy, this time aimed straight at Apollo. He managed to avoid it, but only just.

****

Apollo focused on the air around them. He began to absorb it all, creating a suffocating atmosphere. This seemed to affect the creature, it appeared to be getting its energy from the environment and this was making it lose focus. Apollo continued to absorb all the possible air he could, but he was tiring. Even though this affected the creature, it didn't really stop it. It kept moving towards him. For a second, the creature seemed ready to attack him but quickly shifted his attention back to Amelia, who was still lying in the middle of the road. She was stirring, slowly regaining consciousness. It turned and was headed straight for her.

"Stay away from her!" Apollo yelled.

The creature stopped and turned back slowly. It appeared to inhale once again and released another beam of energy, this time making direct contact. The beam of energy hit Apollo straight in the chest and he was thrown back, crashing hard on the ground.

****

Samantha watched this scene as if in slow motion. A deep rage took over and she found enough strength to get back up. She powered her hands with electric charges and jumped at the creature, placing her hands on its neck and releasing electricity directly into its body. The creature stumbled backwards, trying to pry her grip off.

She felt the creature grow weaker. All the different attacks were becoming more than it could handle. She held on tight, releasing a much stronger electric charge directly into its back. It fell to its knees.

Everything began to heat up around them. A fire had erupted out of nowhere and Samantha saw Amelia standing nearby. She wasn't sure if she was in complete control of her powers, but the flames were becoming stronger and coming closer.

"Sam! I can't control it, get away!"

Samantha released the creature and ran towards Amelia. High flames erupted around the huge creature, closing in, slowly, inch by inch. Amelia's hands were shaking violently.

"I can't hold it for much longer," she cried out.

"You can! I know you can!" Samantha put her hand firmly on her shoulder. "You can do this! I've been wrong about you, Amelia, I know that… I am so very sorry, about everything… You *do* have the power to do this. You *can* control it. I believe in you…"

****

Amelia looked over at Apollo's still figure, laying motionless on the hard ground. She focused, beads of sweat dripping down her face. The flames became brighter, stronger, hotter. She yelled out, the power coursing through her was more than she had ever felt. Heart beating fast, muscles aching, she closed her eyes. Her screams of pain filled the night as bright flames engulfed the creature.

Samantha joined in on the attack, sending another strong electrical charge towards the beast. It let out a horrible sound, halfway between a scream and a howl, and then, after a few minutes, the night air became silent.

Amelia dropped to the ground in exhaustion. The flames disappeared. The creature's body lay still and burnt, its skin charred and melted. Samantha got close to it, making sure it was dead. She left it there and walked back to Amelia. There was a moment of silence, in which Amelia wasn't quite sure what to say. Should she apologise for running away? None of this would have happened if she had just stayed. Once again, she felt like a burden more than a part of the group. Samantha extended her hand to help her up and then they both ran towards Apollo.

"Polo!" Samantha called out as they reached his side. She knelt beside him, checking for a pulse. "Polo!"

"He's not breathing!"

"Como on, Polo, please," said Samantha, she shook his arm.

"Do something!" Amelia screamed.

She took a moment to think. "Alright, just step back," she said as she pushed Amelia to the side.

She roughly unbuttoned Apollo's shirt and placed both her hands flat on his chest. She charged her hands with the necessary energy and released the electricity into his chest. Nothing.

"Try again!"

Once more Samantha shocked Apollo. Nothing, no movement. No pulse. He was not breathing.

"Please, please don't die," said Amelia, tears rolling down her cheeks.

"Come on, Polo," she said. "Please don't leave me, you can't!"

Once again, she charged her hands and released the energy into his chest. Nothing. Again. Nothing. Again. This time something happened. Apollo began to cough and gasp for air. Amelia and Samantha both sat back with relief. Then Samantha moved closer to Apollo and slapped him hard on the face.

"What the hell are you doing?!" he asked, eyes wide with shock.

"Don't – ever – do – that – again!" she said, hitting him hard with every word. She got up and ran her fingers through her long blonde hair. "God, Polo! How crazy do you have to be to do that?"

"Sam, calm down, will you?" Amelia tried to come to Apollo's defence. "He was just trying to help."

"I told you to stay behind!" she yelled. "What were you thinking?"

"You needed help!" snapped Apollo. "Just because you're fine with getting yourself killed to protect us, doesn't mean I have to be okay with it!"

Samantha didn't seem to have an answer to this, she got to her feet and walked back to towards the truck.

CHAPTER FOURTEEN

The next morning Amelia woke up with a very intense headache. The events of the previous night still ran through her mind. She had been reckless and stupid and almost gotten them killed.

The danger surrounding them had never been more real. For most of her life she had been alone, running from one place to the other, only worried about hiding and staying away from people, but never really worried about any one other than her getting hurt.

Now, she worried about the others. They had taken her in, even though she posed a higher threat of exposure, risking their lives for her on at least two occasions now. How many more times would she put them in danger?

She refused to be the weak link. Her powers scared her, yet she knew that if she could learn to control them she could be a great asset to their team, not just a liability. She had seen that last night. She had been able to have a slight control over her power and even generate it with more force than she ever had before.

She climbed out of bed determined to find Samantha and resume their training, hoping to finally show signs of improvement. She got changed and went searching. She went to the kitchen hoping to find them there, but there was no one. She checked their rooms and still no sign of them.

Finally, she found them in the control room. The were sitting in front of a smaller computer screen, whispering about whatever they were looking at.

"Hey, what are you guys up to?"

"Morning, Amelia," said Apollo, smiling widely. Samantha didn't look happy at all. Something was going on.

"Um, Sam, I was hoping we might be able to pick up where we left off – with my training, I mean," said Amelia. There was an awkward feeling of tension in the room.

Samantha just stared at her for a few seconds. "Not today."

"Why not? I know I messed up yesterday, but I don't think that's enough of a reason to stop training me! I promise I'll do better!"

"I'm not saying I won't train you ever again, just not today. There's no need to be so drastic."

"Oh – right," Amelia felt embarrassed.

"Come have a look at this," said Apollo, turning his attention back to the computer screen. "We received an encrypted email a couple of hours ago. We're not sure where it came from or who sent it - but look…."

Amelia walked up to them and saw what they were reading. It was a very short email, you could see that the person who sent this must have been in a hurry. It simply read: *'You have to be prepared for what's coming… time is running out… stay safe.'*

The email also contained various file folders attached. Dozens of folders filled the screen. Each folder contained different files. In one of the folders, the files contained different names and a number. Some of the names on the files were familiar, and Amelia knew why. They were their parents' names. On one of the files she read her mother's name, Kathryn Tupper. Her heartbeat quickened. She knew nothing about her parents. Would these files allow her to know who they were? Why they did what they did? Why they chose to be part of such an evil project?

The one thing she had always wanted was a family. She used to dream that one day, she would be able to find her parents, that they were alive and well and that they would be reunited, and all the time spent apart would mean nothing. All a silly dream, but it had stuck with her. Through her childhood and now as a teenager, she felt silly still hoping for the same thing.

"Have you seen what's in the files?" she asked, trying to keep emotion out of her voice but failing miserably.

"We've just glanced at them," he answered. "We only managed to decrypt the message a few minutes ago. Now I'm trying to find a way to trace it, to see if we can find out where it was sent from or by whom."

Honestly, Amelia had felt little curiosity about anything except her mother's file. She hadn't stopped to think about who could be sending them this secure information. They have no one else, no other ally.

"Do you think it could be a trap?"

"It was the first thing to cross our minds," said Samantha, bitterly.

She was clearly in a terrible mood - for a change – and with no intention of taking it easy on either of them today.

"We have to be very careful with this," said Apollo. "There is no telling who could have sent it or why. It seems like someone wants us to dig deeper into the experiment our parents were a part of."

"Someone just might want to help us."

"There is no one left out there to help us," said Samantha. She ran her fingers through her hair.

"You don't know that," said Amelia, getting annoyed. She thought this might be a good thing, a sign that maybe they weren't as alone as they thought. They didn't need so much negativity, they already had plenty of that. "We don't know how far this goes, or how big it was. There might be some person out there, wanting to help us."

"Or to trap us."

"Don't be so pessimistic!"

"Right, because our lives have always been filled with nothing but happiness and fairy god mothers that help us out." Samantha added, sarcastically. She took a deep breath, "listen, sorry to be blunt, but you know very well that there is no mystery person out there coming to rescue us."

"Maybe –" Apollo began to say, then stopped short.

"What? Come on, Polo, let's hear it. What's your theory, don't be shy?"

"Maybe it was – Alex," Apollo suggested, hurrying his words.

Samantha turned to consider him for a minute. "Don't be stupid, Polo," she said harshly.

Amelia could see she was still upset with him for his thoughtless behaviour from the previous night.

"Alex is probably dead… She's dead and we'll be dead too before you know it! We have no idea how big this is and how unprepared we are to face any of it! You saw that creature last night! We only managed to get out of there by pure luck. What if there are more just like it? It found us, somehow. They are getting closer to us, every day. Alex left us alone, she didn't care about what happened to us! She just left us with no hope. Just come to grip with the fact that there is *no one* out there to help us! We are in this alone and we will be in it alone until we finally get captured to be tortured or killed!"

"Why don't you just shut up, Sam!" Amelia yelled before she could get another word in. "Why do you have to be such a bitch all the time? It's not our fault that you're always so bitter and you think life treated you badly. Finn and Alex didn't leave us because they wanted to, they risked everything for us… Gave up everything, to keep us safe."

"Ames, just stop," said Apollo.

"No! I won't stop! *You* should stop defending her all the time!" Amelia continued angrily. "You know what, Sam? We're trying our best and Polo has a right to be hopeful. If there is even the slightest chance that Alex is alive, I'll take it."

Samantha was quiet for a minute, her face hiding whatever true emotion she was feeling.

"Fine," she finally said. "You do whatever you want. Believe whatever you want. But I'm done. I'm through with trying to teach you and train you for things that you are clearly not ready to handle. And me being a bitch all the time is the thing that's probably going to keep you alive."

"Sam, she didn't mean –" Apollo began to say.

"Don't… She meant every word," said Samantha. "At least she's finally starting to have some guts." She turned around and stormed off, leaving Amelia and Apollo alone in the room. They both stood in silence for a few seconds.

"You really shouldn't be so hard on her, you know," said Apollo.

"You must be joking… Are you really going to take her side? After how she just treated you!" Amelia's voice was high pitched, filled with shock.

"Look, I'm not taking sides," he said. "I just know what she's gone through. It wasn't easy for her, she's had to take care of us ever since Alex disappeared. She's had to be the responsible one, because lord knows we weren't... And then, after they took Michael, well – she was just different, I guess."

"Different how?" asked Amelia.

"Well, she tried to be stronger, for my sake mostly. She pretended not to feel or care about anything. She said that caring only gets you hurt. She lost a bit of herself when we lost him."

"I – I didn't know that she and Michael were so close," said Amelia. She felt guilty about being so harsh before.

"Yeah, well... She's in love with him. Always has been," said Apollo, looking down at his hands.

"I didn't know," she said, feeling somewhat awkward. She seemed to hesitate for a minute and then asked, "But... What about you?"

"What about me?" He asked with a sheepish smile.

"You *are* in love with her, aren't you? I know we joked about it the other day, but I really was being serious, I have noticed how you look at her – what she clearly means to you," she said, as though this was the most obvious fact in the world.

He shrugged his shoulders. "I've never told her. No point in making things weird or uncomfortable between us, you know?"

"Polo –" Amelia began to say.

"It really is okay," he said. "It's no big deal."

"Well, I think you should be honest with her."

"God, no!" he said. "Have you gone completely insane? There is no way I'm ever saying a word to her."

"Why not?" Amelia demanded.

119

"Hmm, let me think," said Apollo, sarcastically. "Oh yeah, maybe because she is already in love with another guy that is a million times better for her than me and she would probably laugh in my face."

"Well, she is kind of a – er… never mind, that doesn't matter," she said quickly. "I don't think she would ever laugh at you for something like that! And besides, you are just as good as Michael. Don't sell yourself short."

"You don't even know Michael; how can you think I'm better?" asked Apollo.

"I didn't say you were better," she smiled at him. "But, seriously, Polo, I may not know Michael as he is now… But I *do* know you. And you are more than enough for any girl. Just think about it, I mean, what's the worse that could happen? And besides, I find it very hard to believe she feels nothing for you. I saw her reaction when she thought she had lost you. There is definitely something there."

Amelia stepped out of the room, leaving Apollo with his head filled with thoughts about much more than just the email. He had never once considered telling Samantha anything about his feelings for her, he had decided it was best for both of them if he never did.

He remembered what it was like, seeing her with Michael. It ate at him from the inside out. Wanting to reach out to her, to maybe let her know on some level how he felt, but he always fought against it. She didn't see him as anything more than a friend and probably never would. Could there be a chance for him? He stared blankly at the computer screen, trying to focus on the task at hand. He clicked a few keys but did nothing of consequence. After a few minutes of this, he seemed to regain his focus.

If he managed to trace the source of this email it could change a lot. If there was some other person out there to help maybe they could become stronger, have a way of not being afraid all the time. The thought of an ally that could allow them to finally defeat Snyde or at least offer some additional support to stand front against a possible fight with the large corporation was more than welcome.

He made a few copies of the files and would hand one each to Amelia and Samantha, that way they could search through them quickly, looking for any clues or any information that could help them in the future. For now, he double clicked on the file that had initially caught his eye. The name read Hailey Stark. His mother. What little he knew about her were distant memories of stories that Finn and Alex had told him when he was a boy. These had started to fade as time had gone by but, there was not one day when he did not stop to think about what life could have been if his mom was still alive. Had she not been a part of the experiments, had they just been a normal family.

Name: Hailey Stark
Date of birth: July 14th, 1968
Status: Deceased
Test Subject: 231214
Last update: April 28th, 2009

Today's session with the subject showed no progress. The subject is weak, refuses to speak and to cooperate with the experiments and tasks set out. Since the children were taken the subject has not spoken more than a few words. The serum has bound well but, without cooperation from the subject we can not progress as we would have hoped. Her mind seems completely lost, she never recovered from the loss of her child. This simple event drove her to insanity. If there are no changes in the next month the subject will be exterminated, and a new subject will be selected.

Apollo stopped to think about what he just read. His mother had stopped functioning the night he was taken from the facility. This stirred up feelings of intense sadness within him. Something he was not used to experiencing. He had always been the positive one. The one who saw the bright side of things, even when it was most dire. All this brought one very important question to his mind. If Finn and Alex would not have taken him that night, could his mother's fate have been different?

He pushed this thought away and continued to scan through the files. He reached another update that caught his attention.

Date: *November 12th, 2007*
   The subject displayed an outburst of her powers today. She suffocated five of our best doctors while they were performing a procedure to bind her DNA to new serum ESH21, which would have given her better endurance and prolonged use of her abilities with less debilitating effects. She became enraged and in less than a minute had taken the life of the five men. She was forcefully sedated and taken to her cell for severe punishment.

Apollo read the words over and over. Her powers had been strong, she bound well with the serums administered but she had been rejecting the experiments, not wanting to participate willingly. He didn't feel like reading any more of this. Knowing how his mother had lost her mind and her life had been ended for the simple reason of not wanting to be a pawn in their experiments, how could this help them at all?

Why did they get sent all these file? His mind was buzzing with an overload of information. He removed his glasses and closed his eyes, trying to clear his mind. After some time, he decided to close the file and leave it for later, he needed to make sense of other things before he could focus on this.

He picked up the two copies he had made for the girls and pocketed them. In the mean time, he had configured a trace that would keep trying to pinpoint the server and location from where the email had been sent. This could give them an actual lead and a real place to search for answers.

He took one final glance at the screens and left to find Amelia. He found her laying in her bed, reading a book and munching on some chocolate chip cookies.

"Is this a bad time?" he asked, knocking on her open door.

"Clearly, can't you see how busy I am?" She answered, sarcastically.

"Nice! I think I'll take a few minutes of your time either way."

He took a seat in the empty chair next to her bed.

"What's up?" She asked with a sly smile. "I hope you're not upset about Sam. I personally think she was out of line, but I know you probably think she was docile and enchanting."

123

"This may surprise you, but I'm not here to talk about Sam."

"I'm only teasing," she added. "Please, don't be offended."

"I'm not, don't stress. I just dropped by to give you this." He pulled out one of the small USB drives from his pocket. "It's a copy of all the files we received. There are files for each of our parents and also hundreds of other subjects that participated in the experiments."

She took the USB and held it the way one might hold a small explosive. "Polo, I'm not sure I want to read these files. I know I should... I'm just worried it would be too much for me to handle."

"I will admit it doesn't act for pleasant bedtime reading," he added jokingly. "But, if you feel up to it, there might be something there that you want to know."

"Did you read any of them?"

He nodded. "I read some of my mother's file."

"And?"

"It wasn't something I would choose to read again."

Amelia put her book to the side and considered this information. "You know what I was thinking?"

"Do tell."

"Well, after everything that has happened to us, what we've been through and what we have to look forward to, we should try to take advantage of any positives in our lives."

"I'm not sure I get where you're going with this."

"Think about it, your feelings for Sam, that's an amazing thing but, you don't want to tell her how you feel, even though if you *do* tell her she might feel the same and you could share something unbelievable."

"Let me stop you right there –"

"No, let me finish," she continued. "I know I'm just a kid and I've never been in love before or had anyone love me but that doesn't mean I don't know how important it is. If I was given the chance I would go for it. You never know if you won't get another opportunity. If she doesn't feel the same, then you'll know and be able to move on… but what if she does? Then you can experience what that would be like."

Apollo didn't have a reply for this. He had thought about this many times before trying to work out every possible scenario and outcome if he ever did pluck up the courage to admit his feelings. In every one of these fantasies it never worked out and she had always said she was not in the same place. Then there was Michael. They were like brothers – however difficult it had been for them to get along. He played a big factor in Apollo not taking a chance. It felt like the ultimate betrayal. Making a move on the girl he loved while Michael was being held prisoner, tortured – or worse.

"Let's just drop the subject. I think it's best, okay?"

She shrugged her shoulders in defeat. "It's your call, but promise me you will at least consider it at some point in your life, before it's too late…"

"Do you really think I haven't considered it? Things never seem to point to the right direction."

"Sometimes you can't wait for something to seem right, you have to take a chance even if you can't see all the benefits. I mean, what's the worse that could happen?"

"I could die," he said. "I mean, literally. I could just drop dead from just the idea of saying it out loud."

"I'm being serious," she said.

"So am I! What? You think I should go over there now? And just let it all out."

"If you put it that way you make it sound like you are headed to meet with your executioner," she laughed.

"You did see her mood, right? It's pretty much the same thing!"

"True. But no matter, that's the person you chose to fall for! It's your own fault."

"Touché," he said earnestly. "Well played. I swear she's not always like this."

"So only ninety five percent of the time?"

"Maybe ninety eight…" said Apollo, a big grin on his face. "Thanks, Ames. I know you're just looking after me. I guess… I might consider it."

CHAPTER FIFTEEN

After his talk with Amelia, Apollo stood in front of Samantha's bedroom door for what felt like an eternity. He was sure he wouldn't have the courage to do this. Nerves were taking over, there was a tight knot in his stomach and he was wondering why he'd eaten so much for breakfast, when now he just wanted to throw it all up. His palms were sweaty. Maybe he shouldn't do this after all.

He thought about Amelia's words, 'What's the worse that could happen?' she had asked him. He knew she was right, but he felt weak and out of breath just thinking about it. It was true, there was no way he could lie to himself, he was head over heels in love with her. But how could he actually put it into words, and say it to her face, no less?

He put his hand to the door and took a deep breath. "Okay, you can do this," he told himself not too confidently. After another couple of minutes, he finally plucked up the courage of knocking.

"Come in," came her voice from inside the room.

He walked into the room and saw her standing at the corner of the room, dressed in black track pants and a top, throwing some punches on the large boxing sandbag, which she usually only did when she didn't want to think about all their problems. She did this a lot lately. Soon he would be giving her one more problem. But Amelia was right, he couldn't keep it to himself any longer, feeling like he was about to implode at any moment.

"Is everything okay, Polo?"

"Yes, everything is fine. I just, um, wanted to know if you had a minute to discuss some things? Or I could come back later if you prefer."

She gave him a big smile. "I've always got time for you. Have a seat. Before you say anything, I wanted to apologize… for what I said before. I was way out of line. It was wrong of me to treat you the way I did. I'm not really sure what came over me. I think, I have too much on my plate if I'm completely honest. It's no excuse, I know that. I've too many thoughts at once. It's giving me a headache to be honest."

"Care to share your thoughts? Tell me about it, maybe I could help. You don't have to carry all the burden by yourself."

"Don't worry, you have your own share of problems, you don't need mine too."

"No, really! I want to know, I want to help."

"I know you do," she said. "You are too good to me, taking into account how moody and aggressive I've been lately."

"We all have our ups and downs," he said.

"That's not an excuse, I've been horrible these past months. I only seem to have downs. It would be nice to have some ups along the way. I know I've been too hard on Amelia and on you as well, but you always stick by me."

"I always will," he looked at her, taking in every detail, how beautiful she was. He cleared his throat, getting back to reality and why he was here. "So, what's been on your mind?"

"Right, well, I can't stop thinking about the files. I keep thinking, maybe Mikey sent it to us."

"Michael? I don't know," said Apollo, turning serious. He really didn't feel like discussing Michael when he had come here to tell Samantha of his own feelings for her.

"I know he isn't the smartest at computer hacking," she continued, "but, Snyde has him and who else could have access to files like those? It has to be someone from inside his labs."

"I guess... But, it's not like they would just give him a computer and say 'here, send some emails to your friends'. I've still got the tracker hack running, trying to pinpoint the exact location where it was sent from. We'll know more once that's finished."

"Yeah, I guess." She sat down, running her hands through her hair in frustration. "Is it stupid of me to think he's still alive?"

Apollo took a seat next to her and put his hand around hers. "Listen, he is definitely alive. And we will get him back. I promise, not matter what happens, we will get him back."

She nodded. "Okay... You're right, I know you're right. It's just hard to stay positive sometimes."

"That's what I'm here for," he said. "Don't forget that."

"I never do," she said. "So, what did you want to talk to me about?"

"Oh, um, I – I brought you a copy of the files." He handed her the small USB. "I thought that you would want to have a read through them whenever you had the time."

"Oh, great. Thanks. I will definitely scroll through these today. You never know what leads could come from them."

"Right... That's what I thought." He was silent. He felt his chest tighten, his palms drenched in sweat. He wiped them off his pants and began fiddling with his glasses.

"Are you sure that's all you wanted to talk about?" She asked. "You're acting a bit odd."

"Me? Oh, well. There was something but, it wasn't really important," he said, the knot in his stomach returning, it was getting hard to breath.

"If it's important to you, it will be important to me."

Apollo hesitated. "I'm just not sure how to say it."

"Well, it's me, you can tell me anything. Whatever it is, I'll try and help."

"Right – this is difficult for me so maybe, so maybe, let me speak and after I'm done you can say what you think."

"Sounds serious… I won't interrupt, I promise," she said with a wide grin. "Just give it your best shot."

He stood up and began pacing back and forth, took a deep breath and began to speak. "Er. Okay, um, here I go. See, I was talking to Amelia before and she told me that I should tell you this… That I should be honest because there is no point in me not saying anything and then I might not get a chance."

"Sounds like smart advice," said Samantha, smiling. "Sorry, I didn't mean to interrupt!" She added at the look Apollo gave her.

"Okay, so um, like I was saying. I – you see there's something that I've always wanted to tell you but the time was never right, I suppose. For a while now – actually, for as long as I can remember – I've had certain feelings. Feelings for *you*… I've tried to get rid of them, I mean, you're with Michael and I know there's probably no chance that you feel anything for me, but I – maybe it was time that you knew… That I was honest with you about it."

Samantha stood up and began pacing the room as well. "Hang on a minute, I'm not sure that I understand. Feelings? I think I'm confused."

"Feelings… as in romantic feelings." Apollo was having seconds thoughts about this, perhaps it had not been the smartest decision, but it was too late to back down now.

Samantha stared at him blankly, she looked speechless. Her eyes wide, probably in shock. He knew Samantha had not expected any of this and probably wasn't really sure how to respond. The seconds of silence seemed to stretch out into hours. Apollo felt sick, his stomach churning, his throat was tight, his palms sweaty again.

"You can talk now," he said. He was taking deep breaths, trying to keep his hands from shaking.

"Polo, I – I think I need a minute." As she walked around the room the lights flickered. "Sorry, I – wow, okay, I just don't know. Are you *sure* about this?"

"Sure, about being in love with you? Yeah, pretty sure. I've had years to think about it."

"Right… Yeah, I can't – I mean, why didn't you say anything before?"

"Well, you were with Michael. It never really felt like the right time I guess. I never believed you would leave him for me," he said uncomfortably.

"Polo, I'm *still* with Mikey." Samantha continued to run her hands through her hair.

He knew he had put her out of her comfort zone. Sharing her feelings was not something that came easy for her.

"Yeah, I know! I just never had the courage to say anything before, alright? I didn't mean anything by it."

"I think I need some time to process all this. It's a bit much."

"Look, I get it, don't worry about it. It was stupid of me to think that you could feel anything for me and I probably shouldn't have said anything to begin with." His tone was changing now, he wasn't nervous anymore, he sounded angry, upset.

"That's not what I'm saying, Polo, but try to understand! It's not fair for you to expect an easy answer to something that is so very complicated."

"It's not that hard! You either have feelings for someone or you don't!" He was plain angry now, not really sure why because this is what he had expected. It hurt more that he had imagined.

"That's not fair and you know it! You know how much you mean to me, you're my best friend! You know how much I love you!" She was raising her voice, shouting the words at him, lights flickering on and off with each word.

"You're just not *in* love with me, I get it."

"I *can't* be in love with you, Polo… I'm sorry, but I just can't. You're such a nice and sensitive guy, I –"

He cut her off, "Don't be sorry, about any of it. And don't worry about me being *too sensitive*. Sorry I'm not an empty headed, narrow minded, shallow, opinionated, strong idiot like Michael. I'm sure he's well deserving of all your attention!"

"I didn't mean it that way, Polo! I just meant – I don't even know what I meant… Please understand, I don't want to be the one to break your heart."

"Yes, well, too late for that, isn't it? You know, Amelia is right about you, you are selfish and cruel and don't care about anyone else's feelings." He turned around and stormed out of the room, not letting her get another word in.

He made his way through the hallway and past the living room, where Amelia now sat on the couch reading her book. As soon as she saw him she knew what had happened.

"Polo, wait! Where are you going?"

He didn't respond, he grabbed his coat and was out the door before she could say another word.

Samantha stormed into the room after him, she was furious.

"Where did he go?" she demanded.

"I have no idea. He just walked out."

"Damn it!" She slammed her hand against the door and a lamp beside the couch exploded, showering Amelia with glass.

"Sorry," said Samantha, trying to calm herself, once again displaying her telltale move of running her hands through her hair.

"It's not a problem," she got up to get a broom and clean the mess. "So… What happened? Are you okay?"

"Not really."

"I don't think I've ever seen you lose control of your powers like that," Amelia said, as she picked up the shards of glass.

"It doesn't happen often."

"Oh, come on, Sam," said Amelia, putting the broom aside and sitting back down. "I know you hate me, but you *can* talk to me if you need a friend. Must be hard sometimes having only boys to talk to."

Samantha considered her for a moment and let out a soft sigh. "I don't hate you. But I'm not much for girl talk, so don't worry about it."

"It won't make you less tough if you *actually* tell people how you're feeling. It's not a crime to be human every now and again. You don't always have to go through everything alone."

Samantha though about this for a moment and then sat down on the couch beside her. "You're not going to want to braid my hair or anything like that, are you?"

"Oh my God, did you just joke with me?! Now I know this must be a dream."

"Am I really that bad to you?" asked Samantha.

"Truthfully, yes, but it's fine. I understand. I'm the outsider who can't control her powers and am driving you insane while you try your best to teach me something. Admittedly, it is not an easy situation."

Samantha looked at her for a minute. "You're not an outsider... It was never my intention to make you feel like you were. I'm really sorry. I shouldn't be so hard on you. This apology is long overdue. I guess the reason for my behaviour is that I know how much potential you have and how amazing you can be, so I don't understand why you're so afraid to use your abilities. It frustrates me."

"You would be afraid of your powers too if you had hurt someone you cared about. I've told you, I don't want to hurt anyone else... I'm afraid with my powers I will."

"You can only hurt people if you don't know how to control them," Samantha said.

Amelia gave her a small nod. "I've caught on to that. I know you're right... I am doing better though, I haven't set anything on fire this whole week."

Samantha started to laugh. "That's definitely an improvement."

"You're actually laughing? Let me call an ambulance! Please don't hurt yourself."

"You're an idiot... Or maybe I'm an idiot. I know what you mean about not wanting to hurt people. I have a very similar fear. Only, I'm just afraid of pushing away the people I care about the most. Apollo and Michael... And you."

"Me? It's good to know you care. You won't push us away by just letting your guard down every once in a while. In fact, you'll probably push us away by being such a cold hearted b –" said Amelia.

"I get it! No need to finish that sentence," said Samantha. "Either way, that's not really true. I let my guard down and that's how Mikey was taken," said Samantha. "And now, I've hurt Polo in a way he doesn't deserve."

Amelia was quiet for a moment. She had never heard Samantha talk about Michael, the night Snyde Corp had taken him. "I know what you and Polo talked about, he told me about his feelings. He knew it was a risk telling you… That you might not feel the same way. It's not your fault. Also, I'm sure that you did all you could to protect Michael."

"I didn't… Mikey was taken because *he* was trying to protect me. I'm the oldest and I promised Alex that I would take care of them, that I would keep them safe. I got careless. Michael and I were dating, and I was bored of the same old routine, so he thought we should do something fun. We went out into the city, went into an old abandoned construction site. We were joking around, it was such a great night. He was showing me a new power, something he thought would impress me… Someone must have seen, it's the only way I can think of them having come for us. They came, too many of them. We tried to fight them off, thought we could escape. But, they kept coming, more and more of them. He told me to run. I should have stayed… I could have helped him. Things could have been different…"

"You did the right thing, if you would have stayed they would have taken you as well. You have done the best you can! You took care of them and protected them, but you can't control everything. Sometimes, things just happen. It doesn't matter how powerful you think you are, you can't stop us from getting hurt all the time."

Samantha thought about her words for a moment. Amelia was right, it didn't matter how hard she tried, she couldn't stop them from ever getting hurt. "From what I hear, you're good at this giving advice stuff."

"Well, I've learned a lot since I was seven."

"I hadn't noticed."

They both sat quietly for a while. Then Samantha asked, "What if he doesn't come back tonight?"

"He'll be fine. Polo can take care of himself, Sam. He's grown a lot too, you simply don't seem to have noticed. He needs some time to himself, he knows he can't force you to be in love with him."

"I hope you're right… Thanks for the talk. I think I'll try and get some sleep."

"I'll finish cleaning up here and wait for a bit… I'll let you know if he comes back."

CHAPTER SIXTEEN

It was half past four in the morning and Apollo hadn't come home yet. Samantha tossed and turned in her bed. It was no use trying to sleep, she was too worried. What if something had happened to him? What if he had run into someone from Snyde Corp and hadn't been able to get way? Every time she closed her eyes she had visions of him captured and tortured.

Exasperated, she got up and went to her desk. She powered on her laptop, inserted the USB drive that Apollo had given her and began to browse the files sent to them. They had received so much information, it would be quite a task to get through it.

She skimmed the files, reading each name. There were a few she felt drawn to and yet, they were the ones she feared the most. Their parents, the volunteers of Snyde's enhancement experiments. She hesitated for a moment and then double clicked on the file containing her father's name.

The file popped open. The first page of the file had a picture of two people who she knew were her father and mother sitting in a white room. There were no distinctive markings anywhere around it. This was probably the first picture she had ever seen of her parents in almost ten years. She wasn't really sure how she should feel about them. They had dedicated their lives to participating in experiments to create human weapons for war. Had they even been good people? Did they think Snyde's methods were the right ones? She would never have answers to these questions, but that didn't mean that they wouldn't always be on her mind.

She stared at the picture for a while before continuing to scan the file. The next page contained a brief description of the experiment and updated statuses by date. She read the first page of the document, which contained the latest information.

Name: Robert O'Connor
Date of birth: May 23rd, 1960
Status: Deceased
Test Subject: 232814
Last update: February 17th, 2001

The test subject's latest tests reveal no improvement. Subject 232814 continues to reject the latest version of the ESH17 serum. His electrical abilities are consuming his organs and destroying his cells one at a time. His body refuses to bind amicably with the foreign cells in the serum. Will not tolerate one more treatment. The most logical course of action in this particular case is for the subject to be sacrificed, he no longer proves a useful asset to this experiment and therefore, is no longer needed for the success of this program. We will schedule his execution for a month from now, leaving enough time to conclude any necessary studies.

Just this first page made her sick to her stomach. She closed her eyes for a minute, thinking about all the horrible things their parents must have gone through. Why had they agreed to participate in these experiments in the first place? Would she find the answers in these files? She ran her hands through her hair and forced herself to keep on reading.

A new subject will be prepared to replace subject 232814. His young daughter has shown promise as a new possible candidate and would undoubtedly serve as a suitable replacement. Her initial bloodwork shows great possibilities. Her DNA has proven to be a perfect binding agent for the serums, even being able to improve them, increasing their level of effectiveness for other future subjects. This must be cleared with Dr. Snyde. If he approves the experiment on a younger test subject, then all will be set to begin.

They had been planning on using her to replace her father in the experiments. This update was written only two weeks before Finn and Alexa had broken them out of the facility. If they hadn't gotten them out, her future would have been as grim as his. She closed her father's file, not certain if she could handle reading any more. She scanned the files and now opened the one labelled Kathryn Tupper. Amelia's mother.

Name: Kathryn Jean Tupper
Date of birth: August 12th, 1965
Status: Alive
Test Subject: 141284
Last update: April 14th, 2008

The test subject is progressing as expected, the latest version of the ESH24 serum has bonded with the subject's DNA with most satisfactory results. Her strength has continued to increase, and her healing ability has also been fortified with this latest version of the serum. Subject still remains the most valuable asset to the program and will be able to commence with phase five of the project. The subject's DNA will be useful for experimenting on other less viable subjects. Her progress has been vital in creating the new and improved War Dogs. Subject 141284 will continue to break all boundaries for further research.

Samantha stopped to consider this information for a moment. So, Amelia's mom showed a last update as a successful subject and her last status said she was alive. Was she still? The file was from 2008, so much could have happened in nine years, but there was a chance, however small that she was still living this nightmare. Maybe they could find her, even save her. Have someone else on their side.

Samantha leaned back in her chair and glanced at the clock on her bedside table. It was 5:23 am. Apollo was still not back. She stared down at her hands, examining them as if the answer to everything might be written in her palms. All the power that coursed through her veins still didn't stop her from feeling so powerless. She created a small orb of electricity and watched it sparkle and fizz on her desk's surface.

All her life, she had tried to take so much upon herself. She was supposed to protect the others and, as far as she was concerned, she had failed miserably. Michael had been captured in an attempt to protect her, Amelia was struggling with her powers and she was not sure what to do to help her overcome her fears. And now, Apollo. She had inadvertently crushed the one person who had always been there for her.

Running her hands through her hair once again, she returned her attention to the files. Perhaps something else would catch her eye and take her mind away from her personal problems for a few minutes.

She scrolled through dozens of file folders until she came across one labeled *recovered recordings*. She double clicked on it and saw multiple files, all sorted by date. One date in particular came to her attention. It must have been a coincidence, but, this day had stayed in her mind because it had been the same day that Alex had told them she knew Finn was dead.

She turned the volume up on her speakers and clicked on the file. At first, all she could hear was static. After the first twenty seconds she was about to close the file when a man's voice finally spoke.

"Are you certain this is a safe connection?"

"As safe as I could manage."

Samantha gasped when she heard the person who answered. She knew that voice all too well. It was Alexa's.

"You know how risky it is to call me. We agreed you would only make contact under extreme circumstances."

"I know… But, you're the only person I trust, Eli," said Alexa.

There was a moment of silence and further static on the tape.

"You don't seem to trust me completely," said Eli. *"Otherwise, you would let me know your location."*

"You know why I can't tell you that, Eli," said Alexa. *"We always agreed that only Finn and I could know. It was the plan, to ensure they would be kept safe. No one must know, not even you, that was the deal."*

"Don't you think the situation has changed?" Eli asked. *"After what happened."*

"Nothing has changed," said Alexa. *"The main concern is still to keep the children safe and hidden. I am going to make sure of it, with every breath left in me."*

Eli cleared his throat. "That is the main concern, it is also mine. Don't forget all that I have lost for this same cause."

141

"I haven't forgotten," said Alexa. "We have all lost, we all compromised and given up many things for this… Eli, please tell me you've heard from him. It's been almost two months."

"Alex… I'm not sure how to say this. I received the news today. Finn's body has been found…"

There was a minute's pause. "How?"

"He was shot, execution style. One clean shot to the head," said Eli. "My men have been working on recovering his remains. I know he would have wanted to be buried back home, with his parents."

"Yes… He would have wanted that," said Alexa, her voice breaking slightly.

"I am deeply sorry, Alex," said Eli. "I know how close you had grown. What you shared."

"No offense, Eli. But I don't think you do," said Alexa. "Finn and I went through so much together, more than even you can imagine. What about Amelia?"

"There is still no sighting of the girl," said Eli. "But we are still looking for her, everyday. We will not stop, I can promise you that much."

"I need to find her," said Alexa. "I've been searching, scanning the news everyday, looking for any signs of wild or out of control fires. She has to turn up eventually."

"Are you certain she could have an outburst?"

"Yes, I know she will," said Alexa. "She's out there, somewhere. Alone and scared. Ever since she was little, she had difficulties controlling her abilities. One day, she will use them and get reported. When that day comes, I will be there to bring her back home."

"I'm sure we will find her," said Eli. "Until then, how are the others?"

"The children are fine," said Alexa. "They ask questions, wanting to understand what happened. Why they were taken from New York and the semi-stable life we had formed. I haven't explained much, only enough to make them feel safe."

"For now, that is all you can do," said Eli. "You know they would be in more danger if they knew too much."

"I know," said Alexa. "They've started at a new school. I want them to have a somewhat normal existence. They deserve it. Michael is into sports, he's been badgering me to let him join the football team. I've told him I'll think about it, but it's too dangerous. He could hurt someone, even without trying. Samantha spends most of her free time in her room, not wanting to talk much, so I guess that makes her a normal teenager."

"And Apollo?" Eli asked.

"Apollo is one of the brightest boys I have ever seen," said Alexa. "So much like his mother, Eli. Kind and giving, always putting others first. He loves to learn and is crazy about technology. There isn't a gadget he doesn't want to play with and learn more about. The kids are growing up fine. I'm trying my best, but… It's all so much more difficult now, without Finn."

"I understand. I wish I could do more. Alex, just promise me, you'll be careful," said Eli. "I know you've been doing this for years now, but I don't know how much longer this hiding in plain sight will be effective for. I've told you before, Snyde's men are everywhere. He has managed to infiltrate so many organisations. Even more than we had previously imagined."

"So, he continues to gain strength," said Alexa.

"Yes, every single day," said Eli. "He works from the shadows. Not showing himself in public too often. But he has gained some very wealthy allies. People who want to be there to claim the benefits when he finally creates his ultimate human soldiers."

"Isn't there anything you can do?" Alexa asked. "You know so much of what he's done, Eli! You could prove so much harm he has caused, you have evidence in your possession to bring him down! I know you do."

143

"We've talked about this before," said Eli, calmly. "If I try to take him down publicly, he will do the same to me. None of us are innocent here. You know my part. Even though I regret it. I live with guilt every day that goes by."

"So, you would rather have others continue to die, than to face the consequences of your own actions?"

"If only it were that easy," said Eli. "You know things are not black and white. You of all people know, I have paid dearly for what I did. But, if I go down, a lot of people will be hurt. You and the children would not be able to have all the facilities you take advantage of now. Don't forget that, Alex. It is my funding that has kept you safely hidden all these years."

"I'm sorry, Eli. I don't mean to sound ungrateful," said Alexa. "I know how much you've lost. I just… I wish things were different. I want to see Snyde pay for all he's done."

"He will," said Eli. "One day, I know he will. We will make him pay for all he has taken."

The recording stopped. Samantha could not believe what she had just heard. Who was Eli? Why had Alex never mentioned him? This was the person behind all their funding. Behind this hideout. Why did she never tell them all that she knew? All those years, she kept so many things from them. All the lies she told over and over. Had it really all been worth it?

CHAPTER SEVENTEEN

Samantha had been so lost in her thoughts she was startled when fifteen minutes later she heard the front door open and slam shut. She bolted from her chair and went to the living room. When she got there, she saw Apollo. He looked terrible. His face was badly bruised, and he had a deep gash across his brow. He had obviously been drinking and got himself in an unnecessary fight.

Samantha frowned and walked up to him. "Where the hell have you been? Do you have any idea how worried I've been?"

"I'm fine," was his only answer.

"Oh yeah, you look amazing!" she retorted. "What happened?"

"Nothing, just leave me alone," he said, walking straight past her, towards his room. She followed him, anger building inside her.

"Is this really how you're going to act?"

"I can behave anyway I want, I don't need your permission! And I certainly don't need to explain myself to you."

"How is it you even look this way? Did you just allow someone to beat you senseless?" She took a deep breath, wanting desperately to calm down. "Let me take a see those cuts."

"I'm fine! Will you stop already? It's nothing that won't heal in a few hours. I'm not a child!" he yelled.

"Well, you are definitely acting like one! Now, just let me take a good look."

"Stop fussing over me, Samantha! I'm alright… I told you, I can take care of myself."

"Fine, I'll stop fussing over you." She pushed him roughly onto a chair. "Just sit down, will you? I don't know what the hell you were thinking!"

"I wasn't! That's the whole point! I didn't want to keep thinking about anything, I just wanted to drink and forget. Forget that you turned me down and that I ever said anything to you about my feelings in the first place."

She didn't speak. He clearly needed to get this out, so she stared and let him talk.

"And then, I wanted to be a normal guy for once, you know? Get into a fight for no reason and be sore the next day, but you know what? I can't even be sore because I'll be fully healed by tomorrow! That's how normal I am."

"Am I supposed to feel sorry for you? You'll still be hungover tomorrow, if it makes you feel any better," she said angrily. "How reckless do you have to be to do something so stupid? Do you have any idea how worried I've been? Do you even *care*? I thought you had been taken or tortured and killed."

"Will you stop being so dramatic?"

"Nice, really nice," she said. "Just take a shower and go to sleep. We'll talk in the morning because I don't think I can keep looking at you in this state anymore."

"Whatever, I'm tired of having to do what you say, you're not my mom and you're not my older sister, so don't boss me around."

"Fine, then just do what you want, Apollo, I'm also tired! I'm tired of caring and worrying so much when you don't even care. You talk and talk about your feelings and how *I'm* the bad guy, but have you ever stopped to consider what I'm feeling and all the things *I* have going on inside? No, you haven't. That's not fair, and I'm sick of it."

"*Not fair?* You know what's not fair?!"

146

"Enlighten me, please!" she said angrily. "Tell me what is so unfair about your current situation."

"Everything! Your turning me down and not wanting to even give me a chance is unfair. You not wanting to be with me when, you know what?" He got up and stood close to her.

"What?" He was so close that she could feel his warm breath on her face.

"I am a really good guy and I would do anything for you and give up everything if you told me to. I have watched you be with someone else all these years and it has killed me and yet – I would still do anything for you!"

"Polo…"

He put his hands gently on her face. "I wish that you would at least give me a chance," he whispered.

"I can't, Polo… I am so sorry… I can't let myself fall in love with you."

"Why not?" He leaned in even closer to her. She held her breath, felt her pulse quicken.

"Because…"

"Because, why?" he leaned in closer still, his face only inches from hers. She was sure he would be able to hear her heart beating.

"Because… I don't think I would ever recover from it. It would break me beyond repair if I ever lost you."

"You won't lose me. I will always be there for you, no matter what. But, my heart aches at the thought of never being able to be with you."

She was about to argue again when he leaned forward and kissed her. The kiss was soft, tender and then it was over as quickly as it had started. She pulled apart from him and took a deep breath. He looked at her, probably expecting a slap in the face.

"I'm sorry," he whispered, his hands on her neck. "I just really needed to do that."

She was silent for what felt like an eternity, just staring at him. Then, she touched his lips gently with her fingers. "Do it again," she said softly.

"What –?"

"Kiss me again."

He leaned forward and kissed her, only this time, the kiss was completely different. It was filled with longing and passion and all the emotions that she knew he had kept hidden for so long. She ran her fingers through his hair, pressing her body closer to his, wanting more of him.

This had taken her by surprise, she had not planned to be in this situation and yet, it felt like right. She was tired of always being in control, of doing the right thing for everyone else. It was time to do something for her, and she was certain that right now this was what she wanted. She wanted him.

As they kissed, the lights flickered wildly across the room. He held her tightly. As she felt him move his hands slowly down her body she knew she was in too deep now, had lost her self control. She decided to completely let go, let him take the lead and, for the first time in a long time, allowed herself to feel.

CHAPTER EIGHTEEN

Samantha woke up the next morning with the feeling of having had a wonderful dream. She sat on the bed and looked over at Apollo, still fast asleep beside her. She couldn't help smiling. Last night had been incredible, she hadn't felt this happy in a very long time and she wanted it to last as long as possible. It would be hard getting back to reality.

She ran her fingers through her hair and stretched out. She didn't want to wake him, he looked so calm and peaceful. She softly touched his face, all signs of bruising had healed now, his skin was smooth. Taking one last glance at him, she got up quietly and got dressed. With one final glance at Apollo, she pulled the door open, smiled to herself and stepped out into the hallway.

She made her way to the kitchen, where Amelia already sat having breakfast.

"Good morning," she said with a grin. "I made coffee, in case you want some."

"Great, thanks." Samantha poured herself a cup and noticed Amelia was staring at her, still grinning widely. "Are you okay?"

"Yes, I'm feeling great to be honest," she answered. "How about you? Did your night finish off better than expected?"

Samantha eyed her suspiciously, there was something odd about the way she was looking at her. "Okay, what is it?"

"What do you mean?"

"You're being weird – more than usual, I mean. You are obviously dying to ask me something, you can barely control yourself."

"I don't know what you mean! I swear, I was just wondering if things had gotten better for you. After all, you were having a pretty tough night, that's all."

"Right. Well, the rest of my night was fine," said Samantha.

She couldn't help smiling at the thought. She looked down at her coffee cup and took a sip, not wanting to focus too much on Amelia.

"I'm glad. Oh, by the way, I'm sure you must have noticed that there was something not quite right with the electricity last night and there are a few electrical appliances not working this morning."

Samantha looked up from her coffee. "Don't worry about it. I'll fix them."

They sat in silence for a while, Samantha drinking her coffee and Amelia picking at the food on her plate, glancing sideways at Samantha every now and again.

"Alright, you're creeping me out. Will you ask me already?"

"Oh, okay, Sam, just tell me what happened with Polo! Did you guys make up?"

"I knew there was something going on in that head of yours," Samantha said. "I'm not sure if that is any of your business."

"Please, tell me! Curiosity is killing me!"

"You are so childish." Samantha smiled at her. "Yes, we made up," she added, with no further explanation.

"I figured you had."

"Why do you say that?"

"I don't know, something about you this morning. You look happy, Sam," Amelia added as an afterthought. "It suits you. You deserve to be happy, even if you don't think so."

"Yeah… Thanks," answered Samantha.

She cleared her throat, not really wanting to get into any details about her incredibly complicated love life. She was ready to change the subject.

"Listen, I've got a different training session planned for you. I think it will help you let go of your fears a bit, help you control your powers with more ease. We could continue tomorrow. Give you today to clear your mind and prepare for it."

"Okay… sure. I'm willing to give it a try."

"There's one more thing," said Samantha.

She had been going through this in her mind last night, going over telling Amelia she had read her mother's file. She had decided it was best to tell her the truth and to mention the possibility of her being alive.

"I was going through our parent's files last night. There's so much information, but there's something that caught my eye about your mom's."

"What was it?" asked Amelia, no longer grinning.

"In all the files there are updates of how each of our parents were reacting to the different serums that were being administered. They were all rejecting the serums, the side effects were killing them… All except for your mom," Samantha finished slowly.

"What do you mean? I don't understand."

"Her file mentions that the serum was binding well with her DNA. She wasn't being hurt by it. It was actually making her stronger. The last update was from 2008, but it was a positive update… She was still alive, back then."

Amelia did not speak immediately, she sat staring blankly at her hands.

"What does this mean?" Amelia finally asked. "Could she still be alive? Held captive?"

"I'm not really sure what to make of it," said Samantha. "Are you okay?"

"Does it say anything about where they were being held?"

"I have to continue reading the files. It doesn't give much detail as to *where* the experiments were held, just about their reactions to the serums."

"If she's still alive I have to save her, Sam!" There was a determination in Amelia's voice that Samantha had never heard before.

"Hey, if there is a chance that she is alive, *we* will save her... Together. I promise."

Amelia nodded and gave her a warm smile. "Thanks. I've got to get better at controlling my powers. I feel like I haven't done enough."

"You're doing what you can. Today is a new day, let's just focus on that for now... Your coffee is really bad, by the way."

Amelia started laughing so hard she choked on her breakfast.

"Mind if I join?" Apollo walked in the kitchen and sat down next to Amelia. He glanced nervously at Samantha who in turn blushed and distract herself by pouring more coffee into her cup.

"Sure! You want some breakfast?" asked Amelia, she got up. "I'll serve you a plate." She stood next to Samantha, with a big grin on her face.

"You're really getting a kick out of this, aren't you?" asked Samantha in what was almost a whisper, so Apollo couldn't hear her.

"I can't help myself, you guys make such a great couple!"

"Keep it down, will you? You have no idea how complicated my thoughts are right now, so can you just act like a normal person for once?"

"I'll give it my best shot but, I can't make any promises."

They went back to the table and finished their breakfast. Samantha was glad that no more talk of last night came up during the rest of the meal, though she couldn't stop the way she felt every time she looked over at Apollo. She could feel butterflies in her stomach. Nerves that had never really been there before. Anticipation of what was to come.

CHAPTER NINETEEN

"There is something I want you both to listen to," said Samantha.

They were all sitting in the control room, wondering why Samantha had summoned them here after breakfast. She played them the recording she had listened to the previous night. After they had heard it, they were silent for a few minutes. Each lost in their own thoughts and not really sure what to think.

"Who do you think this Eli person is?" Amelia asked.

"I'm not sure," said Samantha. "I looked through the rest of the files, but there is no information on who he might be. Or how he was involved with all of this. The one thing we do know, he is the person behind all our funding."

"You know what this means, don't you?" Apollo asked.

"We're not alone," said Samantha.

"Exactly," he said. "I mean, we might be. For all we know, this person might be dead or not even be involved anymore… But, it's a chance."

"I doubt he's dead," said Samantha. "We have never stopped receiving the yearly supply in our storage. He must still be out there, somewhere."

"That's true," said Apollo. "We need to try and find out more about him. But, where do we start?"

"I agree," said Amelia.

"There might be more in these files," said Samantha. "There are so many of them, it's hard to search through everything. Specially through the audio files."

"He seamed to know about us," said Amelia. "Like, he received updates on what we were up to."

"Yes, but there had to be a reason why Alex wouldn't let him know our exact location," said Samantha. "Think about it, if he was her ally, why not just tell him? Why keep us hidden from him?"

The three of them fell silent. It was true, they had felt a jolt of excitement at the thought of not being alone, that out there, somewhere, there was someone who could possibly help them. But there was also the fact that Alex had not trusted this man enough to let him know where they were. They had agreed to the secrecy. Why? Apollo broke the silence with something else that had caught his attention.

"Why do you think he wanted to know about me?"

"What do you mean?" Amelia asked.

"On the recording, Alex was telling him about all of us, he asked about me specifically," said Apollo. "Why do you think that is?"

"Maybe it's just a coincidence, Polo," said Amelia.

Samantha crossed her arms and looked at him. She didn't think it was a coincidence, but she really did not have a clue what this man's particular interest was in Apollo. Perhaps it was nothing, and he just asked for the one child that she had not mentioned. But it was odd, in any case.

"I wouldn't worry about that, Polo," said Samantha. "I don't think it means anything. He might have asked about any of us if she had mentioned you first."

"We have to keep scanning these files," said Amelia. "There must be a reason they were sent to us."

"Have you considered the fact that they might have been sent to us to try and trace our location?" Samantha asked.

Apollo looked at her and nodded. "I've been thinking about that ever since we got the email. But, I've put up so many firewalls. I don't know what else I can do to prevent someone hacking us."

"Don't forget, these people are a lot smarter than us," said Samantha. "They must have more technology then we can even dream of. What if accessing these files can lead them to us?"

"Sam, I don't think –" Apollo started to say.

"Do me a favour," interrupted Samantha. "For now, let me be the one to scan through the files. You just make sure that you are monitoring any strange activity in our networks. We have to be vigilant."

"If you think that's best," said Apollo.

"I do, at least for now," said Samantha.

There was not much else to say on the matter. Anything they could say was just guess work.

"Is there anything I can help with?" Amelia asked.

"You can go down to the training room and keep working on your powers," said Samantha. "I have a feeling, now more than ever, it is vital for you to get a handle on them, the sooner the better."

"No pressure," said Amelia, smiling.

"None at all," said Apollo.

"Just, get some practice and then get some rest," said Samantha. "Tomorrow, we can start the new training session."

Amelia nodded and left the room, leaving Apollo and Samantha.

"Sam, just remember that you don't have to take all this on by yourself," he said.

"I know," said Samantha. "I'm not trying to, really. But, I think it's best if we share tasks. Divide and conquer, you know?"

"Alright," he said. He gave her hand a squeeze and watched her walk away.

****

That evening, Samantha sat at her desk, scrolling through the hundreds of files that remained. There was information on many different subjects, not just their parents. So many more people had participated in this experiment. Had they all suffered the same effects as they had? Were these people out there, with powers of their own?

They had never heard Alex speak of any more people with abilities like theirs. She had always said they were unique and their powers had to be hidden, because the world was not ready to see something so amazing. People fear what they did not understand, and therefore, they would all be in danger.

They were still in danger, even without the world knowing about them, but it would be an even more dangerous place if they were not careful. As she double clicked on the next file, a new recording began to play. This one was different, it was not a conversation between two people. It was an audio log for one of the experiments.

"Subject 231214," said a woman's voice. "Stark, Hailey. Third procedure. A new serum will be administered. Her progress will be closely monitored. Her initially weak and infected cells have regenerated successfully. She no longer shows any signs of disease. Her body is stronger than ever before. With this new version of the serum it is expected that the subject will begin to display signs of additional abilities."

"Stark, Hailey," said Samantha, under her breath. Apollo's mother. She ran her fingers through her hair, anxious about what could be on this file.

There was a pause and the sound of something being wheeled into the room.

"How do you feel this morning?" The woman asked.

"I feel stronger," said a new woman's voice. "And yet, parts of me feel strange. Like they don't belong to me anymore."

"This new voice must belong to Hailey Stark," Samantha said to herself.

"Don't worry," said the first woman. "It is only logical, with all the changes being made to your DNA structure. You are bound to have a period of adjustment."

"Will Finley be here to oversee the procedure today?" Hailey asked.

"No, today I will be the only one here," said the first. "Now, please lay still. I must strap your arms and legs. You know the procedure, this will be painful."

Samantha waited as the recording went silent. She thought there was nothing more, but the time on the audio file had a few more minutes to play. She waited, listening intently. After two minutes she heard a scream that startled her, almost knocking her off her chair. It took her a few seconds to realize what had happened.

They were administering the serum and it was causing such intense pain that the only noise in that room were the most blood curling screams she had ever heard in her life.

"Stop!! Please make it stop!" Hailey yelled out in pain. "I can't – Don't – It's too much! Please! I beg you – Stop!"

As another horrible screamed filled the room, Samantha stopped the audio. She could not sit there and listen to this much pain. It was unlike anything she had ever imagined.

Then, something happened that made her jump up from her chair. Even though she had stopped the recording, she continued to hear screams. She quickly realized that these were not coming from any file, but from inside The Bunker. She ran frantically out of her room, in search of the source.

CHAPTER TWENTY

Rain drops were falling everywhere around her. She could feel the cool water against her skin, making the hairs on her arms and back of her neck stand on edge. Amelia scanned her surroundings. She was on a rooftop. It was late at night, only a few apartment lights remained on. There was something so familiar about this place, yet she could not put her finger on it.

She was dreaming again. Something about her dreams scared her. They were becoming more frequent, each time the scenery around her seemed clearer. Like she was watching a film. Watching, unable to interact or change the outcome.

She turned as a man spoke.

"Don't move," she heard a man's voice call out.

As she turned towards the sound she again saw a familiar face. Finn. He was standing in front of three armed men, all taking aim directly at his head.

"Where are the kids?"

"They're gone! Far away from here, you'll never find them," said Finn.

"It's no use lying, if they are nearby we will find them," the second man said. "If you tell us where they are, we might even spare your life."

Finn didn't speak.

"Are you really willing to risk everything for this?" The men walked closer to where Finn stood. The first man pushed him to his knees and put his gun agains't Finn's forehead.

"You have one last chance. You would be smart to take it, I'm not usually this generous. Just tell us where the little brats are, and you can live."

"Do whatever you want with me," said Finn, his voice surprisingly calm. The man pressed his finger against the trigger but stopped suddenly as a woman's voice spoke.

"Wait," the voice was calm but full of authority. The man looked sideways at her and frowned.

"What are you doing here?" he snarled at the woman as she came closer.

"Now, now, Saunders," she said in a perverse tone. There was something dark about her voice. "I would have thought you would be simply thrilled to see me. After all your past failures, Oleander did not want to risk one more, so he sent me along to *assist*."

The man called Saunders backed away still glaring at the new arrival. She turned her attention to Finn.

"How wonderful to see you again, Finley. Specially since you are where you belong... on your knees," said the woman.

A deafening bang resounded across the night sky and then all was quiet.

****

"Ames! Wake up, Ames!"

Apollo rushed to her side, trying to wake her. She tossed and turned in her bed, not responding. She was clearly lost in a nightmare that had a tight grip on her. Her hair was stuck to her face, drenched in sweat. Small fires started bursting to life around the room, quickly consuming anything they touched.

"Amelia, I need you to wake up now!"

He reached over and shook her arm. Her skin was burning hot. He flinched in pain. His hand had burnt at even that slight touch. Fear was creeping in. He needed to wake her up or else there was no telling what damage could be done.

Samantha ran into the room. She looked around at the scene with a sense of dread.

"Polo, what's going on?"

"I heard her screaming out," said Apollo. "She won't wake up. She's not in control of this."

"Start the sprinkler system manually from the security room," said Samantha, the urgency in her voice made him act quickly. He ran out of the room.

Samantha looked on as the small fires became more intense. There was nothing she could do to stop them spreading. As she considered her options, water started to fall from the ceiling. The fires slowly began dissipating and Amelia awoke with a start as the cold water hit her face.

She sat up in bed, startled and gasping for air. She was disoriented. Images of the rooftop clear on her mind. She scanned the room quickly and realized she was safe, sitting in her own room in The Bunker.

She saw Samantha looking at her and felt worried.

"What happened? What did I do?"

"You were having a nightmare," said Samantha. "We couldn't wake you. Fire started spreading in your room. We set of the sprinklers to stop them. It was the only way we managed to wake you."

Amelia realized that there were tears in her eyes, mixed with the water from the sprinklers.

"I'm so sorry, Sam," she said. "Please, don't be upset."

Apollo came running back into the room. He reached Amelia's side and hugged her.

161

"I'm so glad you're okay," he said. "You had me scared for a moment. You were in a trance. No matter how many times I called out your name, I couldn't wake you."

"I'm alright," she mumbled.

Her eyes were set on Samantha, afraid of the effect this could have on their new budding relationship. It had only just started to improve.

"Amelia," said Samantha. "I'm not upset. I'm concerned about you."

"We both are," said Apollo.

Amelia looked from one to the other. She knew they were being honest. They were genuinely concerned for her. She had not told them about her dreams. About these things she was seeing. First the fire at the grocery store, now the rooftop. She was certain these were not just dreams. They were memories. From a time long ago. Things she had seen as a child but had blocked in the deepest part of her brain.

Perhaps it was her new circumstances that were forcing these memories out. Being here, with the others. The fact that they all wanted answers. They wanted to understand their past.

"I – I've been having these dreams," said Amelia. "I had one the other night, when I ran away. Before that monster attacked. And now this one. They've been so real…"

She recounted what she had seen and how vivid it had all felt. How she observed but was unable to affect the course of her dreams or interact with anyone in them. She was a third party spectator, nothing more.

They both listened intently. Once Amelia had finished speaking she sat in silence, looking down at her hands. A few tears still in her eyes. She felt guilty. She thought about the fire in the grocery store. That's what had caused all this to happen. If it had not been for that, perhaps Snyde Corp would never have found them. They could have had a very different life. They might all still have been together, growing up in New York, like they had been for years.

"This has all been my fault," she whispered.

Apollo looked at Samantha, who shook her head.

"No," she said. "This was not your fault. None of it is. There is no one to blame. Things happen and there is nothing anyone can do to change them. It's just the circumstances under which we have lived. You were just a child. Any of us could have had an incident that could have alerted them, at any given time."

"You have to stop blaming yourself," said Apollo. "Sam's right, it could have been any of us. We were never going to be safe."

"The only person to blame here is Snyde," said Samantha. "He's the one who has been out to destroy us our whole lives. We have made it this far without getting caught, and we will keep going. As long as we can, whatever it takes. We can't give up."

Amelia looked at both of them and smiled. She was grateful that they did not blame her. Despite everything, she had never felt more at ease. They were right. There was nothing she could do to change all that had happened. She just had to focus on what was to come. On her training and being able to overcome whatever was in store for them in the future.

"Um, not to mention the obvious," said Apollo. "But, I think you're going to need somewhere else to sleep tonight."

He looked around the room. Everything was wet and covered in soot from the fires. Amelia laughed as she in turn scanned the room.

"You can stay with me tonight," said Samantha. "After that, you can take Mike's room. At least, until we clean this one back up for you. Then, tomorrow we can continue training."

Amelia nodded and wiped the tears from her eyes. She forced the images from her dreams out of her mind, deciding to worry about the here and now and not about things that had passed and could no longer be changed.

CHAPTER TWENTY ONE

Michael awoke with a start, unsure of where he was. His arms and legs were restrained, as usual. He felt weak, not having eaten for days. Once again, they were punishing him for breaking the rules. He had managed to escape his prison briefly when a guard had brought his meal. Instead of trying to leave the facility – which he knew was suicide – he had tried to gain access to a computer and send the others a message, but it had been useless. He had been recaptured and now was in a higher security confinement.

Total darkness, he could not see the colour of the walls or know if there was anything else in the room with him. He was shackled and bound, his hands tied to the ceiling, his ankles to the floor. His arms ached, from hanging from their restraints. Despite the ability to heal rapidly, he felt tired, drained and in constant pain.

He closed his eyes and thought about the one thing that kept him going. The only reason he had not simply asked to die. Samantha. She was still out there, he had to get back to her. He thought about the last time he had seen her. It had started off as any normal night. Just the two of them. They had gone for dinner and a movie. Trying, as always, to have some fraction of a normal life.

He could still remember everything about that night. The way she looked, a small navy blue dress that complimented her delicate figure, her long blonde hair in waves resting over her shoulders, her deep blue eyes sparkling in the moonlight, her lips full and delicate. He couldn't forget the way she smelled, a mixture of fresh flowers and vanilla. Her laugh, soft but joyful at the same time. There was nothing he wouldn't give to hold her again. To kiss her and let her know how much she meant to him.

Regrets of his behaviour that night still played on his mind. He had been childish. After going to the movies, they had walked to an old abandoned building that had been left under construction. The construction site had been left with debris, rocks, construction equipment. The money had run out and everything had been left untouched.

The view from the top was amazing. Always the best place to catch a sunset or a sunrise. They had gone to the top to gaze at the stars. They had sat, huddled close together, his arm around her shoulders. Thousands of stars sparkled in front of them, lighting the night. A full moon was out, making everything much clearer.

"I've been thinking," he had said. "Why don't we go somewhere? Just the two of us."

"Like where?"

"Anywhere," he said. "You're always saying how it would be great to travel, that all your friends from school have gone away. Maybe we should too."

Samantha looked at him but did not answer.

"We can travel, go anywhere in the world," he continued. "There is nothing stopping us."

"We can't just pack up and leave," said Samantha. "We have responsibilities."

He had stood up and begun pacing back and forth.

"I don't get you," he said, his tone turning angry. "Why do you always have to act like the weight of the world is on your shoulders? Why do we have to take responsibility for things that weren't even our decisions?"

"It is because of those decisions that we are still alive and safe," said Samantha. "Alex always told us about our past, how they rescued us. How we got split up. We are still here because they were brave enough to care about us. We have to do the same. We must keep looking for Amelia. She's out there somewhere."

"How do we even know that? What if she's living an amazing life out there? Maybe she found a family where she fits in and doesn't even need us?"

"Mikey, you're being selfish," she said.

"I'm not, honestly," he said. "I'm just trying to think about what I want, for once."

"I think that's the exact definition of selfish," she said, grinning.

He looked at her and smiled.

"So, what if I am? Don't I have the right to want things for myself?"

"You do," she said. "But life isn't that simple. Not for us, at least… Then there's Polo."

"What about him?" he asked, a hint of jealousy in his voice. "He's a big boy, he can take care of himself. You're always looking out for him. Why do you always have to make him an excuse?"

"I'm not! But we can't leave him alone," she said. "We are the only family he has. I don't know what's come over you. Why the sudden need to get away?"

"It's not sudden," he said. "I've felt this way for years. I just never thought it was the right time. There was always something holding us back. Now that Alex is gone, I just thought that we could finally make our own way."

"Do you even hear yourself? It's not like Alex decided to simply move out. She was taken, she's probably dead."

Michael looked ashamed of his behaviour.

"Look, Sammy, I didn't mean it that way. I just feel frustrated sometimes, you know? I wish that life could be different. That's all."

He walked closer and kissed her softly.

"I'm sorry," he said. "I don't mean to be such a jerk sometimes."

"Sometimes?" Samantha teased.

"Fine, maybe all the time," he said.

167

"It's fine," she said. "Let's just drop the subject. Maybe when things get less complicated we can think about travelling."

"There are so many things I want for us," he said.

"I know," she said, smiling. "So do I. I hope we'll have time."

He nodded and reached for her hand.

"Look, there's something I've been practicing," he said. "I wanted you to be the first to see it."

"What is it?"

He directed her attention to the open sky in front of them. Stretching his hand out, a small water sphere began to form in front of them. It grew larger and larger as he focused on it. As the sphere grew, it began to spin and swirl around itself, forming different shapes and small waves within it. The water slowly began to change density and turned into solid ice.

"Mikey! That's amazing!" Samantha exclaimed. She stood to inspect the sphere.

He grinned, clearly proud that he had managed to impress her.

"I've only just managed to get a hang of it," he said. "I still have a lot to improve on."

"Still, this is so wonderful," she said.

He turned his attention to the sphere and it floated up above their heads, breaking itself into thousands of small pieces that fell on top of them, like snow flakes. They sat for a few more minutes, watching the tiny flakes float around the evening sky. It had been magical, until, without warning, all hell broke loose.

Shots were fired, striking Samantha in the back and causing Michael to jump to his feet and pull them both behind cover.

"Sammy! Are you okay?" His voice was panicked.

"I'm fine," she said, cringing in pain. "It's nothing, it will heal in no time."

He looked at the spot where the bullet had entered, just below her left shoulder.

"What's going on?" Samantha asked.

He looked around and saw, a few feet away, three armed men walking towards them, all covered with thick armour. He focused on the first one and sent out a huge stream of water his way. The man was thrown backwards, and the others ran behind two stone pillars, seeking cover of their own.

"Snyde Corp," he said.

"How did they find us?"

"I don't know," said Michael, trying to make sense of their situation.

"You don't want to fight us," one of the men called out. "We have this building surrounded, you have no way out."

Michael risked a look down and saw the man wasn't lying. Down below he could see movement. They were coming for them from all directions. He had to do something to get them out of this one.

"Sam, I want you to go," he said, seriously.

"What?! No way! We are fighting them together," she said. "We are both getting out of here."

He shook his head.

"Trust me. There are too many of them. I won't let them take you."

"Mikey, please! This is ridiculous! We are stronger together."

He hesitated but nodded his head in agreement.

"On the count of three, we step out of cover and take them on, one at a time," he said.

She nodded as he whispered the countdown. On three, they began their attack. Both jumping out of their cover, each taking out one of the guards.

He took her hand and they ran towards the broken stairs down to the next floor. More guards came their way, they easily dispatched them. Samantha aimed electric bolts towards two more guards coming their way. They were descending the remaining steps and would soon be out onto the ground floor and into the street, where more guards awaited.

A slew of gunshots was fired their way as they stepped out into the open night. Michael sent a well-aimed attack at four men to their right, while Samantha took aim at another to their left. No matter how many men they had taken out, more seemed to be coming.

Michael felt a piercing pain in his leg and fell to the ground. He looked down and saw a fresh wound, gushing blood. Samantha knelt to help him up. More shots came their way. Michael got to his feet and saw two trucks racing towards them. He pushed Samantha to the side, but he was not so lucky. One of the trucks rammed into him hard, sending him rolling to the ground.

"Mikey!"

He could hear her calling his name, but everything was in chaos. His ears were ringing, his vision blurry.

She reached his side and put an arm around him, trying to lift him.

"No," he mumbled. "Run... Go, Sam... Save yourself."

"No, please, we can take them," she said.

"They're too strong," he said, holding his ribs in pain. "Sammy, please. I'll hold them off. Just run! Please, go!"

He pulled himself to his feet and with all the remaining strength he could manage, he let out a violent attack on the men approaching them. He created sharp ice spears, that penetrated one of the armoured men, who to the ground, dead.

"Go, Sam! Run!"

She finally did as she was told and ran. She glanced back at him, just as he felt a sharp pain in his neck. He reached over with his hand and felt a small dart. He instantly became dizzy, his hands felt heavy. A sedative dart. The night fell silent.

He remembered coming to in a strange room, needles and cables attached to his arms, strapped to a table, doctors prodding him. He had been unable to use his abilities, they had placed a power cancelling ankle bracelet on him. Since that day, he had been experimented on, tortured for information, beaten until he lost consciousness.

Snyde had not held back on the force that was to be used against him. He knew that no matter what, Snyde would use him for what he wanted, even if it ended up killing him. He was disposable, but not yet. There was still something he needed. A piece that was missing for his final experiments.

Michael still had not understood everything about Snyde's outcome, but he knew that there was a special serum being developed. A serum that was different to the previous ones. It mattered more to Snyde. Michael also knew that to make this serum he needed samples of their blood – all four of them.

He had to find a way to warn the others, to keep them safe. A part of him wanted the others to rescue him, but the other more rational part knew they had to stay as far away from Snyde and this facility as possible.

CHAPTER TWENTY TWO

After breakfast, Samantha led them to the big training room once again, only this time, when Amelia stepped into the huge open space, it was completely empty. There were no targets, no candles, no mannequins, no hanging sandbags, like there had been on all the previous occasions.

Amelia was puzzled. What was this new technique that she was about to try out. Maybe it was just trying to not burn the place down.

"Okay, today I'm giving you something simple," Samantha began. "Polo, stand to one corner please, and whatever you do, don't interfere."

Apollo nodded and went to stand out of the way, he crossed his arms in interest, looking just as puzzled as Amelia felt, but he didn't question her instructions.

"So, what am I supposed to do?"

Samantha didn't answer. She walked towards the centre of the room and stood there. "Like I said, it's simple. You are going to concentrate on creating a ring of fire around me."

"Excuse me?" asked Amelia, clearly she must not have heard correctly.

"You heard me, create a ring of fire around me."

"Um, Sam…" Apollo began to say but she held out a hand to stop him.

"You can do this, Amelia. You can't be afraid anymore, there's too much at stake. Every day we will be in more danger. Snyde will never stop searching for us and I believe that for some reason he really wants *you*.

It was made clear to me the night the creature came after us. He wanted you, more than us. If you don't learn how to control your powers and rely on them, you won't stand a chance against anything he can throw at you. And I won't always be there to protect you."

"But, what if I hurt you?"

"You can't hurt me, trust me."

"You're being awfully smug," said Amelia.

Samantha laughed. "It's not about arrogance. I trust you."

"Polo should at least put a forcefield around you."

"No, Apollo won't be doing anything. It's just you and me now."

"I can't! Are you insane? You've seen what I've done to the targets, can you imagine what I can do to you? It's too powerful, I can't control it."

"Yes, you can! Believe in yourself. Close your eyes," Samantha instructed her.

Amelia very reluctantly did as she was told.

"Good. Now, listen to the sound of my voice and nothing else. Clear your mind. Take a deep breath and exhale slowly."

Amelia complied. She tried not to think about anything, even though it was hard. She had so many things to worry about. David, her mom, Snyde being so intent on capturing her, hurting Sam, hurting anyone. She took a deep breath and slowly tried to push all that from her mind.

"Okay, now focus on the energy that you feel flowing inside of you. It's not a curse, Amelia, it's a part of you. Don't be afraid of it. You have to stop thinking about it as a bad thing. It's who you are, it will always be inside of you. Feel it coursing through you, from your heart, all the way to your fingertips."

Amelia once again did as she was told. She focused on all the energy that had always been there, coursing through her. She had rejected it on countless occasions but now, she tried to make room for it. Something strange was happening inside her. She could feel the fire, but it wasn't controlling her, it was flowing with her, all the way down to her finger tips. Her hands felt hot, but she knew this time she could control it. This time she could picture what she wanted it to do, how she wanted it to flow.

"Open your eyes," said Samantha.

Amelia slowly opened her eyes and saw her hands were shining with bright orange flames. "I did it! I'm controlling it!"

Samantha smiled. "Now, for the fun part. Focus on getting the fire to surround me. Remember, don't be scared… I know you can do this, you won't hurt me."

Amelia nodded. Something inside told her it would be okay. She wasn't going to hurt anyone.

"Ready? Here I go."

She concentrated, sweat dripping down her forehead. Bright flames started forming themselves around Samantha. They burned brighter and brighter until they finally formed a complete circle around her.

"That was brilliant!" said Samantha.

"I did it!" Amelia shouted. She ran over to Apollo and hugged him. "Did you see that?"

"It was great," he said. "I always knew you could do it. I told you, you just had to believe in yourself."

"Okay, now just make the fire extinguish," said Samantha.

"No problem," said Amelia.

Once again, she focused, concentrating with all her might on the fire. She felt as the heat from the flames seemed to go back into her body. All the flames disappeared from the room, not one trace of fire remaining.

"That wasn't so hard, was it?" asked Samantha, a big grin on her face.

"Thanks so much, Sam! For everything, I couldn't have done this if it wasn't for you." She was ecstatic, she felt better than she could remember.

"Yes, you could have. Now, we need to practice as much possible. You have to keep perfecting it, making it as natural as breathing."

"I'm ready."

Amelia practiced on targets for another two hours while Samantha and Apollo sat and watched.

"You're really helping her out, Sam," said Apollo. "This means a lot to her."

"I know, it's about time she started feeling comfortable with who she is. Besides, I need to know that if anything should ever happen to me that you'll both be able to look after each other."

"You say that a lot lately." Apollo was serious. "Nothing is going to happen to you, Sam. I won't let it."

"I know that. But if something *does* happen, she has to be ready. And so do you. I've been trying to keep you safe my whole life. I've been shielding you from the world when I should have just been preparing you to face whatever comes."

"You know I can take care of myself," Apollo reassured her.

Samantha nodded. "I know. Will you stay with her a bit longer, I've got something I want to take care of?" She got up to leave but Apollo took her hand.

"Sam... About last night, I –"

She cut him off. "Not now, Polo. Please, we'll talk about it later tonight. I promise, just not now." Her tone wasn't harsh. It wasn't of annoyance, but there was something there. Perhaps sadness.

"Okay," he nodded, he didn't want to push her into a conversation that would make her uncomfortable. "I'll see you later tonight."

She left the room, Apollo staring after her.

"Where is she going?" Amelia asked.

Apollo shrugged his shoulders. "No idea. She didn't say, and I didn't want to pry."

"Oh… Well, I think I've done enough for today. I'm exhausted." She sat down next to him. "Is everything alright between you two?"

"I think so. We'll be fine, don't worry about it."

"Aren't you glad you took my advice? I told you she had feelings for you!"

Apollo smiled at the thought of the previous night. It had been amazing, but he knew there was something going on inside Samantha that she couldn't share with him yet.

"I am glad I told her, no matter what happens now. I don't think I would change what happened for anything in the world."

"That's great to hear. Are you hungry? Because I am starving! How about some lunch?" she asked him. She was in such a good mood right now, she just wanted to eat and enjoy the rest of her day.

"Sure, how about we go somewhere nice and celebrate. Looks like you won't be burning down buildings today, we should be able to let you out into the streets."

"Funny, very funny," she said, punching his arm. "Come on, I'll take a shower, get changed and we'll go."

CHAPTER TWENTY THREE

Samantha sat in the debris of the old unfinished building. The construction on this particular place had halted at least five year ago, to her knowledge. The cold floor felt familiar. She had been there countless times before, but this was the first time alone.

For years, she and Michael had sat here together and gazed out at the night sky. It was peaceful, no one would come here. The construction site had been deemed unsafe, so people stayed away.

Samantha inspected the area, noticing how nothing had changed since the last time. Running her hand against one of the pillars where bullet holes were still embedded in the cold stone.

Taking a seat on the building ledge, she gazed at the sky, soaking in the changing colours of the incoming sunset. Without realizing it, a few tears had run down her cheek. Samantha did not wipe them away.

It was hard to describe her feelings. She missed Michael, no matter what. What happened with Apollo had brought a new joy into her life. One that she had not felt for so long – perhaps ever. But, it felt like it was a betrayal. It was a struggle, not wanting to feel this way, but not being able to help it.

She closed her eyes and memories filled her mind, of times that seemed so long ago. Recalling one of the first times Michael had brought her here brought a smile to her face.

He had gotten in trouble at school, which in all honesty, was something that had happened all too often.

"I swear it wasn't my fault this time," said Michael. He flashed her a huge smile. "The other guy had it coming. He was picking on two freshmen, they had no one to defend them."

Michael was just a sophomore but well built for his age. He was bigger and obviously stronger than anyone else in his year. Samantha was a junior and tried as much as she could to not get involved in anything that could bring trouble. Michael was the opposite. One way or another, he was always getting into trouble.

"So, *you* clearly had to defend them? You had no other choice?" Samantha could not help but smile back. "You do understand that we're meant to keep a low profile, right? It will never be a fair fight for the other guy. No matter how much you want to justify it."

"So, you expect me to just turn my back? Walk away?"

"Yes, actually, I do," said Samantha. Even though she was trying to keep a straight face, it was difficult. "You act like you don't know what could happen if you draw too much attention to yourself."

"I doubt Snyde is keeping up with the Fairfax High School news," he said, sarcastically.

"It's not about that," said Samantha. "And you know it. If one of these kids ever tell their parents that you beat them to a pulp, they might call the cops. The real ones, and who knows what trouble you could be in. They could even mention how you seem to have super human strength – or how you never seem to bruise after a fight."

"You're pulling at strings," he said. "It's all very unlikely. Besides, they never land a punch, so that's why there's no bruising."

` "Mikey, please. Try to stay out of trouble. It doesn't really take that much of an effort to behave."

178

"What's the fun in that? Oh, come on, Sammy," he said. "If anything, I thought you would be the only one to understand. That's why I told you about it."

She took a deep breath.

"I can't say I understand why you keep picking fights," she said. "But, I understand the need you have to stand up for others who can't do it themselves."

He gave her a wide smile.

"You won't tell Alex, will you? She won't be too happy about it."

With a sigh, she shook her head. "I won't tell her. You would never hear the end of it. And she'll ground you, for at least a year."

"Until Christmas, at the very least," said Michael.

They both laughed. After a few minutes, they fell silent. Michael inched himself a bit closer to where Samantha was sitting. She felt butterflies in her stomach as he inched nearer. There was something she had wanted to do for some time now but had never worked up the courage to and right now, this seemed like the perfect opportunity. Without thinking about it too much, she leaned over and kissed him.

She had caught him completely off guard but, to her surprise, he did not pull away. He reciprocated the kiss and when they pulled apart, they were both blushing deep shades of red.

After that day, things had changed between them. Michael had become the one person who had looked after her, as she had for him. He had always been tough, difficult to handle, over confident and a bit too arrogant. But, with her, he was not these things. He had always put her first.

She opened her eyes and was brought back to where she sat alone. The sunset had passed, and hundreds of stars filled the sky. More tears had freely streamed down her cheeks. It reminded her of that night, when they had been ambushed and he had been taken.

A long time ago, when she was in her rebellious teenage years, Alex had come to her room for a talk. They had a talk about Finn that applied very much to how she was feeling now. Alex had said: *"one of the hardest things in life is learning when it's time to let go. Whether it's letting go of people or places, it is never easy to move forward. We feel uncertain about how life will go on. Change is scary, daunting. However, sometimes, it was the right thing. The only thing that would allow you to move forward."*

Sitting here, Samantha knew for her that time had come. What she was feeling now for Apollo, it had changed her perspective on a few things. She had to take advantage of this chance to be happy once more.

She was never going to give up on finding Michael, but the time had come for her to move forward with her life. He would want her to be happy.

"I'm sorry, Mikey," she whispered into the night. "I hope you can forgive me, one day. But, it's time for me to let go… I'm ready to let go."

CHAPTER TWENTY FOUR

Oleander Snyde wasn't a man who liked failure. He would not tolerate it and would certainly not forgive it. He paced back and forth in his office. How could there be no new sign of the girl? They had let her escape too many times and now, the fires had stopped. The other two had taken her and somehow managed to keep her hidden.

He was growing tired of this. He needed her for the new stage of his plan. There was strength in her powers that even she did not understand. He had severely punished all those involved in letting her escape the last time. Killing meant nothing to him, they were worth nothing.

He had released his Behemoth in hopes that he would be able to find them but, he had not returned from his search, perhaps something had also gone wrong. He had no way of knowing, he had not marked him with a tracker, not finding it necessary for such a powerful creature. Maybe this was another mistake, brought on by arrogance on his behalf. He slammed his fists on the hard wooden desk where he sat.

Now, he was presented with another annoyance. Someone had broken into his control room and sent out various restricted files. He knew who they had been sent to, but the email address could not be traced and the person who committed this infraction had covered their tracks well. He had still punished everyone he thought could have been involved.

The boy, Michael, had endured the most severe punishment. He would recover from his wounds, but this made it even more enjoyable. To inflict the greatest of pain and have that person ready the next day for further pain. When he had first been captured, Snyde was sure that after a few days of such intense torture he would give away the other's location. But now, more than a year later and after daily torture he still had not said a word. No matter how much they harmed him he would not crack, nevertheless, he was still valuable. One day, the others would come looking for him, they would try to save him and then, he would finally have them all.

He picked up the phone and quickly dialled a number. After three rings the person finally answered.

"Hello?"

"It's me," he said into the receiver. "I've grown tired of this chase. I need you to lure them out of hiding. I know they have been trying to hack through our systems. Let them. I'm done waiting. Bring them to me and I will end this myself."

"Yes, sir," was the only answer.

He put the receiver down. This game of cat and mouse was going to end soon, and he would have what he wanted. The power to destroy all those who had ever stood in his way. He would have more power than any other man on earth. And once he unleashed it, no one would be able to stop him.

****

Amelia sat alone in the living room that night. Apollo had already gone to bed and Samantha still wasn't back from wherever she had gone. She was focusing on lighting and extinguishing a few candles set on the table across from her. So far, everything was going great. No out of control fires, no damage to any of the furniture. Today had definitely been her day.

She had had such a great time with Apollo at lunch, she only wished Samantha had joined them. If only she knew what was going on with Samantha, maybe she could help. But Samantha was such a tough person, she never wanted to talk about it.

Amelia lit the candles then with a wave of her hand, turned them off again. Her mind completely blank.

"Having fun?"

Amelia let out a loud scream and one of the candles melted away in a small burst of flames. She had been so focused on her candles that she didn't even hear Samantha enter the apartment and sneak up behind her.

"Don't do that!" Amelia clutched a hand to her chest. "You almost gave me a heart attack."

"Sorry," she took off her coat and went into the kitchen. "Is there anything to eat? I'm starving. I haven't had anything all day."

Amelia got up and joined her. "You should have come with us, we had a great time."

"Maybe next time," Samantha replied as she rummaged through the fridge for something to eat. She pulled out some leftover pizza. "Care to heat this up for me?" she asked jokingly.

"Maybe next time," Amelia answered. "You can use the broken oven in the meantime."

"Is that still not working?"

"Yeah, must have short-circuited the other night."

"Let me take a look." Samantha put her hand on the oven door and it sprung to life. "There, all fixed." She gave Amelia a big smile.

"So how was your day? Must have been busy, you didn't even have time to eat."

Samantha tossed the pizza inside the oven. Amelia could tell she was distracted.

"Listen, I was wondering, do you think tomorrow you could help me work on my fighting?"

"Hmm? Oh, sure, no problem. We can do that tomorrow," Samantha said.

"Great, thanks. I figure it's not just enough to control my powers."

"Sure…"

Amelia watched her fiddle around the kitchen, opening and closing cabinets.

"Can I help you find something?"

"No, I'm… I'm actually not looking for anything. I don't know what I'm doing."

"Are you on something?" Amelia asked suspiciously.

"No! I'm just trying to not think about some things."

"Okay, grab a seat. Tell me what's going on."

"Another girl talk session? Two in two days, must be my lucky week."

"No offense, but it looks like you need one," said Amelia. She pointed Samantha to a chair.

"Fine," Samantha huffed. "You know I'm not good at this. I don't like talking about feelings."

"I know, what was it you said 'feelings just get in the way of other more useful thoughts'. I'm pretty sure it was something like that."

"Close enough."

"Well, like it or not, we all have feelings and at some point, you have to talk to someone about them or you'll go insane. If you don't want to talk to me, at least talk to Polo."

"I can't talk to him about this," said Samantha. "He's probably the last person who would want to hear it."

"Then I'm your best bet – or your only option if you want to think about it that way," said Amelia, cheerfully. "Come on, let it out or I'll make you more coffee."

"Please, don't. Anything but that."

Amelia laughed, "Fine, no more coffee, I swear. Now, shoot. I'm all ears."

Samantha took a deep breath and began to speak. "Today, I went back to the place where Mikey was taken. I don't really know why, I just thought I might be able to sense him… That somehow, I would be able to feel if he was still alive. It's stupid, I know."

"It's not, Sam. Not at all."

Now Amelia understood why she couldn't talk to Apollo about this. Samantha was upset about Michael and Apollo would most likely be jealous or angry, specially after what had happened between them.

"Anyway, I just sat there for hours. Thinking about all that's happened. He's been gone for over a year now and I know I can't hold on to him forever, even if we do get him back… I went there, because I felt like I needed to let him go, and that would be the perfect place. But, I don't know what he… I mean, what he would feel about me and Polo," said Samantha, running her hands through her hair.

Amelia reached over and gripped Samantha's hand, squeezing it tightly.

"Then there's Polo," Samantha continued. "He thinks that I'm this perfect girl and really, I'm everything *but* perfect."

There was a moment of silence between them.

185

"You love them both, don't you?" asked Amelia.

She felt sad for Samantha, not really being able to imagine what was going on inside her head. Samantha nodded, she wiped away a few tears that were forming in her eyes.

"This is so frustrating! I do love them both. But, I can only be in love with one of them. And I can't bear the fact of having to hurt the other."

Amelia hesitated before asking, "do you know which one you're in love with?"

"You're not making this any easier," said Samantha, she smiled. "Look, don't worry too much about it. I'll be alright."

"I know, you're always alright."

"Maybe I'll end up hurting both of them and they'll be fed up with me, that'll make it easier," Samantha joked.

"Good plan," said Amelia, sarcastically. "Listen, no matter what, I think you could never disappoint either of them. And Sam, I do believe Michael is alive. He's alive and we'll get him back. And my mother as well. I really believe things can work out for us."

"Maybe you're right," said Samantha. "I'm exhausted." She closed her eyes.

"You just didn't get much sleep last night."

"Okay, thanks for the girl talk, this is as far as we'll get tonight," she gently slapped Amelia's shoulder and got up, taking the pizza from the oven. "I think I'll eat this in bed."

"You enjoy. I'll keep practicing for a while and then go to bed."

"Good night," said Samantha. "Er, thanks for the talk, Amelia. I do appreciate it."

"Anytime... Get some rest, I'll see you tomorrow."

CHAPTER TWENTY FIVE

"You're really getting better," said Samantha. She was slightly out of breath. "You just have to keep training. It's all about being constant."

"You still beat me every time," Amelia told her grumpily.

"I've been doing this a lot longer."

They both sat down on the large floor mat they had been using for combat training. They were drenched in sweat and exhausted. Amelia was definitely getting better at this, and, at controlling her powers. They had made a lot of progress in the past couple of days. Hopefully, things would just keep looking better from this point on.

"Have you seen Polo this morning?" asked Samantha.

"No, he's probably still in his room. He's still trying to track where the email came from. Apparently, he hasn't made much progress and it's driving him crazy."

"I can imagine. I've been reading more from the files. It's so much information, but nothing seems to actually reveal where the experiments were taking place."

"What can I do to help?" asked Amelia.

"Just keep training. I have a feeling that soon we'll need all the strength we can muster. I'll be back, keep practicing until then. I have to go talk to Polo for a minute."

Amelia nodded. Samantha got up and walked out of the room. She reached Apollo's bedroom and knocked. There was no answer. She knocked one more time, still no answer. She very slowly opened the door.

"Polo? Can I come in?"

Samantha stepped inside the room. Apollo was sitting on his desk, fast asleep on his laptop. He must have been up most of the night trying to hack the location. She closed the door and walked towards him. He always seemed so peaceful when he slept. She smiled, gently stroking his hair. He started awaking.

"Sam, hey," he said, stifling a yawn.

"Hey, sorry to wake you. Any luck?"

He looked at the screen, checking any new progress. Nothing.

"No, nothing new."

"It's okay, it's a long shot really. We may never be able to track the source."

"I should be able to," he said. "Is everything okay? Did you need something?"

"Everything's fine," she said. "I just wanted to talk. I promised we would last night, but when I got back you had already gone to bed."

"Oh, right… You know, we don't have to if you don't want… Um, I – there's no pressure, really, I –"

"You're babbling," said Samantha. "I know there's no pressure, and I *do* want to."

"Oh, okay. Only if you're sure. But, before you say anything, I wanted to apologise. I was selfish, and I never stopped to really think about what you were feeling, and I expected too much from you – then there's Michael, and –"

Samantha gently place her finger on his lips to stop him from talking. "I'm not here to talk about Michael. I'm here about *us*. You and me, Polo. You have nothing to apologise for. Trust me, you weren't being selfish, you had every right to tell me how you felt. I'm glad you did. That night meant more to me than you can ever imagine. *You* mean more to me than you can imagine. I was unsure then because… I don't ever want to be the one who hurts you."

"And now?"

"Now, I want give us a try," she told him, taking hold of his hand. "You're the one who brings my walls down. I feel different when I'm with you."

She leaned forward and kissed him. There was that feeling again, of letting go, of being happy and not worrying about everything that was going on around them. She wanted so badly to hold on to this forever, to forget all their problems. Deep down she knew that sooner or later reality would catch up to them. She could lose him. She pushed this thought out of her mind as he kissed her neck.

"Polo —"

He stopped to look at her.

"What's wrong?"

"Nothing is wrong, that's the thing."

"I don't think I'm following."

She gently ran her fingers through his hair.

"That night when you opened to me and told me how you felt, I was terrified. I knew that I couldn't run from it any longer, from how I felt about you. I also knew what I was risking. I can't bear the thought of losing you, it would tear me apart."

"You will never lose me," he said, gently kissing her forehead. "I know you worry about what will happen, but there are things that no one can control, we can only try our best to live in the now. And right now, I want to enjoy this time with you."

He leaned over and kissed her once more. She relaxed into the moment, losing herself into him, needing more with every second their lips touched.

"We really should go help Amelia," she said begrudgingly, after a few minutes.

"She should be fine for a few hours," he said.

"She could still burn the house down."

He laughed. "We would have time to escape, in that case."

She took his hand and lead him out of the room. "Don't worry, we'll have plenty of time to continue this tonight."

"I like the sound of that."

****

As the days passed on, Amelia continued to show more and more progress. It was like she had become a totally different person. Confident, stronger, happier. She felt at ease, no longer worrying about her abilities hurting the ones she cared about. She finally felt comfortable in her own skin, comfortable with who she was. There was still a long path to travel to reach her full potential but, this was certainly a good start to it. Even her nightmares had started to abandon her.

There was a different feeling in the house. After so many years of suffering, running and hiding, there was a certain peace and, even though they knew it might not last for long, they were determined to enjoy it.

"Sam, have you got a minute?" Amelia asked as she knocked on her bedroom door.

"Sure, I'm just getting ready. Polo and I were going for dinner. You're welcome to come, if you'd like."

"I'm good thanks, I think I'll pass on being the third wheel today."

"Suit yourself," said Samantha, with a smile. "How do I look?"

She was wearing a knee-length, backless, red dress that fitted her body as if it had been made for her. Her long, blond hair came down in waves over her shoulders.

"Amazing, as always," said Amelia.

"You're too kind," said Samantha. "What did you want to ask me?"

"Well, I was wondering, maybe tomorrow we could hang out?" asked Amelia. "I know you've been busy with the files and Polo but, if you had some free time, I could really go for a girls' night."

"Girls' night?"

"I know it's not your favourite thing in the world, but, we could watch a movie or something. I promise to not talk about *feelings*."

"I'm sorry, Amelia. I realize I have been dedicating a lot of time to other things, now that you don't need me to train you as much. I promise we can do something tomorrow."

"Okay, great!" Amelia smiled.

As Samantha finished getting ready they heard Apollo call out.

"Sam! Ames! You should come see this!"

"Great, what's wrong now?" Amelia asked.

Samantha shrugged her shoulders and let out a heavy sigh. "Good question. Come on, let's go have a look."

They found Apollo sitting in front of his laptop, the screen displayed at least five different alert messages.

"What is that?" asked Amelia.

Apollo was quiet for a minute, then answered.

"It's the results of the trace I've been running on the email from our unknown friend. Its pin pointed a location from the server where it originated."

They were all silent. This was the information they had been waiting for, and now that they had it they weren't quite sure what they wanted to do with it.

"It's in North Carolina," said Apollo.

"That's not that far," said Samantha.

"What do we do now?"

"We have to go," said Samantha, determination in her voice.

"No! We have no idea what could be there!" said Amelia.

"I know what's there," said Apollo.

Amelia turned to look at him.

"I've just been doing a thorough check on the coordinates, I've checked satellites and the details of the building registered at the address," Apollo continued. "It's where Snyde's lab is, where all his experiments were carried out. It's where we were born."

"Are you sure?"

He nodded, "I'm almost positive."

All three looked at each other, trying to figure out what the other was thinking. Amelia broke the silence first. "So we definitely can't go," she said. "It's what he wants. He wants us back there, under his control."

"Sam? What do you think we should do?" asked Apollo, turning to look at her.

"We should go," she repeated.

"What?" asked Apollo and Amelia, in unison.

"We'd be walking straight into a trap. That's the only reason for something like this. Why else would we have received that email? Think about it, it's all been a trap from the very beginning. Are we just going to walk right into it? He knew we wouldn't stop until we found the source and now we are going to be playing his game. It's madness."

"Okay, then I'll go by myself," said Samantha.

"You'll get yourself killed!" said Amelia.

"No, I won't. He doesn't want us dead, remember?"

"It hasn't been for lack of trying," said Apollo.

"Oh, *I'm* sorry, you're right," said Amelia, sarcastically. "He won't kill you, he'll just capture and torture you, what a relief."

"Look, we have to do something. What if it isn't a trap? What if there is actually someone in there who is on our side and is trapped."

Amelia saw the expression on Samantha's face and knew what she was thinking.

"Sam, you think Michael could be there?"

"I – I don't know, but it's a pretty good possibility."

Amelia paced the room. "Do you think – my mother could be there too?"

They both looked at her, not saying a word.

"I know that it makes sense for us to try and rescue Mikey or anyone else who may want to help us. I believe that this is where they could be being held. We need to try," said Samantha.

"It's going to be dangerous, we need to have a plan," Apollo pointed out. "It's not like we can just go up to the front door and knock."

"How do you suggest we plan?" asked Samantha. "The more time we waste, the less chance we have of them still being alive."

"Sam, I understand how you feel, but –"

"No, you don't," Samantha cut him off before he could finish. "You have no idea how I feel about this. Mikey was taken because of me. I was unable to help him. If we finally have a location where we can search for him then I have to go."

"What if he's not there?"

"I don't care," she answered. "I have to do something. We've been hiding for too long, waiting for the day when Snyde would find us. We can change that, make the first move and have the upper hand."

They had spent so long training, always thinking of playing defence, perhaps it was time for a bit of offense. If they could infiltrate Snyde's lab they might be able to rescue Michael and do a bit more damage to whatever plans Snyde has.

"Alright, Sam, let's do it," said Apollo.

Amelia nodded her head a bit reluctantly. She still wasn't one hundred percent confident in her powers.

"But if we're going to do this, we're all in it together," he said. His expression was serious, almost defiant. "You have to let us play our part."

"Polo's right," added Amelia. "You can't do everything alone. You need to let us help."

Samantha looked hesitant at their words. Amelia knew what could be going through her mind. If they got hurt – or worse – Samantha would never forgive herself. But, on the other hand, she had to be realistic that she could not do this alone.

"We go together, and we'll come back together," she said. "All of us. We have to get Mikey back."

"So, when do we leave?" asked Amelia.

"There's no point in waiting," said Apollo. "We should go now. Ames, you take care of packing supplies, food and money for the trip, Sam and I will pack any weapons and gear that could be useful."

Amelia nodded and left the room.

Apollo stood next to Samantha and held her hand. "We'll find Michael, I promise. I will get him back to you."

"Polo, it's not about that – I – you know how I feel about you."

"I know. I also know what *he* means to you. Feelings like that don't just go away," he said. "You look amazing, by the way." He let go of her hand and walked out of the room.

CHAPTER TWENTY SIX

The location of the lab was less than a half day's drive from The Bunker. They had spent half their lives so close and never known it. Hidden in plain sight, close enough for Snyde to have found them at any time, and yet he never had. Perhaps this was how things were meant to play out. Them searching for Snyde, not hiding anymore.

Their time had come to prove what they were capable of. Snyde had created them to be weapons and now, they would be used against his own facility, to bring down the empire he had built.

Before they left The Bunker, Apollo had managed to infiltrate the computer servers at the lab once the trace hack finished. He had found the computer from which the email was sent and remotely hack into the lab's facility. With this, they hatched a plan, however rough, it was all they had.

The plan was to reach the lab. Once there, Apollo would once again hack the computer system, gain control of the security cameras and buy them enough time so they could sneak in undetected and search for Michael. Once they had him, hopefully, they could escape without ever getting caught. That was plan A. Plan B involved simply improvising and fighting their way out – or die trying. Admittedly, Plan A was what they were hoping for, as they weren't too keen on dying any time soon.

It was late now. Almost no other cars were on the road with them. They remained silent most of the way, each thinking about what was going to unfold. They were about to risk everything. The realization that they were greatly outnumbered, were so young and lacked experience hit them like a ton of bricks.

Amelia was trying to keep her head filled with positive thoughts, although every two minutes they turned to visions of everything going terribly wrong and of different ways in which they could fail. She kept visualising each of them in a cell, chained and tortured. Each time these thoughts entered her mind she forced them out. She repeated over and over that it would be fine, that somehow everything would work out.

Apollo's thoughts were more focused on what he had to do. Hacking the security system was their best chance of getting out unharmed, he was confident he could do it. He had to make sure this was the one thing to get right, even if other things failed. If the security systems were under their control, then they would be facing less danger.

Samantha's mind kept travelling between imagining Michael being dead or alive. He had been gone for over a year. What guarantee was there that he was still alive? If she was risking all their lives for nothing, she would never forgive herself.

"Get off the road up ahead," said Apollo. "There should be an unmarked exit to our right."

After a few minutes she saw the exit he mentioned. It was easily missed unless you knew you were looking for it, there were no signs marking it and the road was unpaved. You could drive by with no problem at all. It was reminiscent of the road leading to their own hideout.

They drove for another twenty minutes and then they saw it. A large perimeter fence that encircled every inch of the property. They parked the truck far from the fence and would continue on foot to be safe.

Apollo pulled out his laptop and began typing commands, trying to get into their security system as quickly as possible. Every second was valuable for them. Amelia and Samantha stood by, watching him work while inspecting the perimeter fence.

"How are we getting in?" asked Amelia.

Samantha stared at the fence in front of her and felt a very distant and forgotten memory make its way back to her.

"The same way we got out the first time," she answered.

For a while all they could hear was the sound of computer keys being quickly pressed. After only five minutes Apollo spoke.

"I've got it! I've programmed the security footage to run on a loop so whoever is keeping an eye on the camera's will have no clue that we're here."

"Are we one hundred percent sure about this?" asked Amelia, a tone of panic hidden behind her words.

"Let's say I'm ninety nine percent sure," said Apollo.

"That's good enough for me," said Samantha. She took a deep breath and looked at the others. "This is it, no turning back now."

Apollo and Amelia both nodded. "Let's do this."

They walked slowly towards the fence, each step bringing them closer to danger. When they reached it, they stood quietly in front, listening to the low humming sound it emitted. Samantha closed her eyes in deep concentration, focusing on the immense perimeter fence towering over them. In seconds, the fence began to vibrate, and light blue sparks shot out of it.

When Samantha had absorbed all the electricity from the fence they were safe to make their way through. She stepped through first, signalling the others to follow once she had determined it was safe.

"Remember, we don't know what we'll find there, so we have to be careful at all times."

"Constant vigilance?" said Apollo, with a grin.

"Just be alert."

"Are we just going to stroll up to the main entrance?" asked Amelia.

"Not exactly," said Apollo. "We're going through the lab's underground entrance."

Amelia's face showed confusion.

"Trust me, I know how to find it," he said.

"Polo can sense differences in air pressure, regardless of how subtle they are," Samantha clarified. "With his powers, he is able to detect the slightest changes in the air around us. He can find any entrance that will lead us to the underground tunnels, where the air is denser than up here."

"Oh, sounds so – er – simple, I suppose."

"Lead the way, Polo."

He nodded and immediately focused on the task at hand. It took a while and a few failed attempts, but eventually they came up to a hidden metal door on the ground. A trapdoor. There was a keypad in the middle with a red light indicating that the door was locked. Apollo leaned over it and pulled a small device from his pack. He placed the device on top of the keypad and automatically it tried different combinations. After five minutes the light next to the keypad turned green and the trapdoor opened.

Behind the trapdoor was a ladder that led to a dark corridor below.

"I think we need a light. Ames?"

Amelia stepped towards the ladder and focused. She closed her eyes and small flames erupted from her hands. She directed the flames down the ladder, resting them on the bottom of the tunnel, lighting the way for them.

"Okay, let's go."

They climbed down, one at a time, checking their surroundings once they had reached the bottom. It was eerily calm and quiet. They were in a tunnel-like corridor, the walls made of jagged rocks. Humidity hung in the air, making it difficult to breathe. Sweat dripped down their faces from the overwhelming heat, their clothes sticking to their backs.

The trio continued down the cavernous passage. It was very narrow at certain points, forcing them to crouch and practically crawl through. The intense humidity made them feel weak and disoriented. It took twenty minutes to find the end to the tunnel. When they reached it, their path was blocked by another large metal door, locked with a keypad. Apollo quickly hacked it open. When they stepped into the next room, they were surprised to find the environment completely different then the passage they had just been in.

Fresh air struck their faces, clearing their heads instantly. They stood in a clear, spacious room, with shiny white walls and high ceilings. It had the essence of an empty hospital. There was an eerie calm, making the situation quite unnerving. The new room branched out into three different hallways, each with the same gloomy, empty feel of being in a very macabre and sombre maze. The three halls were lined with multiple doors, security cameras at the front of each one.

"I guess it's safe to say that my hack of the cameras worked."

"We would definitely be surrounded if it hadn't," said Samantha.

"Now what?" asked Amelia. "Something doesn't feel right about this place. It gives me the creeps."

"*Nothing* feels right about this place," added Apollo.

"We can't stop to think about that now," said Samantha, firmly. "We have to start searching for Michael. We don't have much time."

"Do you want to search each of these rooms?!" asked Amelia, in a shocked tone. "There could be hundreds or thousands of rooms down here. It's too risky!"

"What else do you suggest?"

No one spoke, each of them trying to figure out what the best course of action was.

"We have to get moving," said Apollo. "It's not like we're going to find an information booth to guide us in the right direction."

"This will take forever," said Amelia. "We should split up."

"No way," Samantha argued at once.

"That's not a bad idea," said Apollo, seriously.

"It's the worst idea I've heard so far," Samantha retorted.

"Come on, Sam, you know it's the smartest thing to do. We can cover more ground that way."

"We don't have any way of communicating or knowing if one of us is in danger and needs help."

"Look, I know you think we can't take care of ourselves, but we can. We are all in this together and you have to trust us."

Samantha knew there was no way she could win this argument. It was two against one and she didn't have time to convince them. Apollo was right, she had to trust that they could take care of themselves. There was no more room for overprotection. It was smart to split up and cover more ground.

She hesitated for a moment and then begrudgingly agreed.

"We'll split up," said Samantha, "but we have to have some rules to this. We search for one hour, if we can't find him during that time we meet back here, agreed?"

The other two nodded. They all took a deep breath and headed towards each of the three corridors.

"Good luck," said Amelia.

"Please, try not to get yourselves killed," said Apollo, forcing a smile.

Amelia took off down the right hand corridor. Apollo was going to head down the middle one, but Samantha pulled him back.

"Polo, wait… There's something I need to say."

"Is this really the right moment?"

"We may not get another one. There's something I need you to do for me, something I need you to promise, before you go."

Apollo saw the serious expression on her face and the tone of her voice. He knew her too well, she was about to ask for something that he could not possibly agree to.

"I need to know that if something were to happen and you had to save yourselves and leave here without me, that you will do it."

"Sam, there is no way," he protested. "We are leaving this place together, that's not negotiable."

"It's not about negotiating. I'm not saying that something bad will happen. But, Polo, please promise. If it comes to a choice between saving yourselves or me, please just promise – you *will* leave me behind."

"You have no idea what you're asking of me."

"I do, trust me. But, I need to be sure that you will be safe. It's the only way I'll be able to do this."

Samantha took hold of his hand, her blue eyes pierced through his own. She was pleading with him in a way he had never seen before. He considered her for a moment before nodding his head in defeat.

"I promise."

She moved closer and hugged him tightly. There was something about the hug, it was as if she was trying to transmit as much feeling as she could into it, as though she would not have another chance to show him how strongly she felt about him.

When she pulled apart, he gave her one last glance and they each began to walk down their assigned corridors, not sure what to expect once they reached the end of it.

CHAPTER TWENTY SEVEN

Apollo walked slowly into the long, white corridor. Each footstep he took reverberated inside his chest. He wiped the sweat from his brow. It was getting very hot – or perhaps it was just his nerves.

Down his hallway, there were ten different doors, seven on the left side and three on the right, each guarded by a security camera and individual security locks. He approached the first door on his left and hacked the lock. The door slid open and he stepped inside.

There was nothing of apparent interest inside the room. It was very small with just some unimpressive lab equipment. He stepped back into the main corridor and tried the second door. Again, nothing.

He repeated the process for a few more doors with no success. There was a definite feeling of anticlimax after searching the first few rooms. Either this was all being too easy or there was something going on that they still had not caught on to. He decided to try the first door on the left side. As soon as he stepped inside his jaw dropped.

He stood in a giant archive. Filing cabinets lined every available inch of the walls and multiple rows filled the room. He began to walk between them, quickly scanning the labels.

He stopped in front of a random cabinet and pulled on the handle. It was locked. That was no issue, it was only a simple key lock. He focused on the small keyhole on the cabinet and expanded the air around it, making it come loose with a small popping sound.

He pulled open the first drawer in the cabinet and scanned the files. There were at least two dozen different files, each with the first name initial and last name of a person. No name stood out to him in this drawer.

He walked over to another filing cabinet and repeated the process. Scanning through these files could take weeks or months, there were so many. He wasn't really searching for anything in particular, he was simply interested by all the information that could be contained in here.

All the experiments Snyde had been working on, test subjects, side effects, all the different powers that could be out there. If only he had time to read each of these individual files. He quickly pulled out drawer after drawer, keeping and eye out for anything that stood out. After fifteen minutes of searching he finally saw a file that made him hold in his breath.

He quickly pulled out a thick file labelled Clarke, M. "Michael." The file contained information about the different experiments that were being conducted on Michael. There were also photos, showing him at different stages since being captured.

Apollo shuffled through the photos and felt a knot in his stomach. One picture showed Michael strapped to a gurney, his arms and legs tied down, needles stuck all over his body. Another showed him laying on the floor, his entire body showed deep cuts, blood puddled on the floor around him. A third photo had him chained to a wall, probes attached all over his chest and what appeared to be drip IVs attached to both his arms. Each picture showed a different injury, each one from a different date.

All this time, they had been torturing him. Each time they had drugged and beaten him almost to the verge of death. Apollo knew that after a few hours Michael would have healed and then, the torture must have begun all over again. He felt sick from looking at these, but he had to keep going, maybe something here would hint as to where they could find him.

One of the photos, that showed him with deep gashes and bruising all over his back, was dated from two weeks ago. He had to be here, they had to find him. He didn't deserve to be living through this hell. Apollo took the file, put it in his bag and walked out, back into the main corridor.

He continued to quickly search the remaining two doors but found nothing that could be of use to them.

****

Nothing appeared notable about the first few rooms that Samantha had stepped into. Lab equipment, empty rooms and a couple of storage rooms. Something felt eerie about this facility. Even though she knew that Apollo had hacked the cameras, everything seemed too still. Too quiet, as if this place was abandoned.

She reached the ninth door. Another empty room with a single door on the other end. She walked towards this new door, put her hand gently on top of the keypad and shot a small surge of electricity directly into it, disabling the locking mechanism and allowing the door to slide open.

In this new room there was a single staircase leading down. She quickly ran down the steps, taking two at a time. When she reached the bottom, she was faced with yet again another door, however something looked different about this one.

"How many doors does this bloody place have?" She mumbled, annoyed at not making any progress in her search. Hopefully the others had found more useful things.

The first thing that caught her eye about this door was the size. It was much larger than all the previous ones. The second difference was that there was much more than just a keypad securing it. Next to the keypad was what appeared to be a retinal scanner and underneath that a hand scan.

Getting past the security measures wasn't what worried her, it was what could be behind all this. So much security for this particular place meant that it guarded something more important. Was this the place they were looking for? Could they have Michael behind this door?

She focused on all three scanners and rendered them useless with only a thought. The huge door slid open. Taking a deep breath, she stepped into the room. There was a loud bang and instant pain to her thigh.

Samantha stepped out of the way as soon as she could, trying to understand what had happened. She found cover behind a desk to her right and examined her injury. Her pant was slowly soaking up blood where a bullet had just pierced her. She was not alone, someone had been waiting for her to step inside.

She could hear steps coming closer. She forced herself to not focus on the pain but on her surroundings instead. Risking a glance, she saw a man approaching, a machine gun gripped tightly in hand, ready to fire. One guard was no problem for her to handle, but were there more hiding around the room ready to shoot as soon as she made a move?

There was no choice, she had to risk it. She quickly stepped out from her cover and sent a jolt of electricity towards the guard. The hit stopped him instantly. He collapsed to the floor, unconscious.

More shots ricocheted around her. The bullets missed by only inches. Samantha took cover again, this time, behind a gurney that was knocked on its side on the left side of the room.

"We've got you surrounded!" a male voice called out. "Surrender now and no one else gets hurt."

For obvious reasons, she did not believe a word he had said. She checked her leg; the pain was subsiding as her body began to heal. Her cover didn't allow a good viewpoint of the room, there was no way for her to know how many men were waiting to take a shot. She had to do something – and fast.

"I feel like I've heard this before," she called out, trying to buy some time.

She closed her eyes, deep in focus. She wanted to create enough electricity to knock out every person in the room but still not enough to cause any real harm. She was not prepared to kill – not even Snyde's men. It required a huge amount of effort to get the balance just right. As the electricity coursed through the room, computer screens and other devices began to explode, shrapnel and debris falling to the ground.

Once she stopped, the room fell completely silent. Samantha stepped out from her cover and looked around. A few guards lay in the floor unconscious, at least ten of them had been waiting for her. That meant Snyde must know they were here. This was a trap and the others could be in danger. She had to go back for them. As she turned, a set of heavy steel bars slammed shut, blocking her only way back.

She was being pushed onward, to an almost certain trap that awaited her. Was she really going to play into this? There was no other way, her hand was being forced. The time had come to show what she was really made of. She walked past all the debris and guards scattered on the floor and made her way to the only exit.

She disabled the lock and the door slid open. Taking a deep breath to prepare herself, she took one last look around and stepped inside. She had walked into a dark room, unable to make out her surroundings made her uneasy. Taking a risk, she created a small orb of electricity to shed some light. It was a large, round room with various barred gates spread throughout.

High above she could make out an upper balcony protected by thick glass. As she inspected the room closer she noticed blood stains all over the floors and walls.

What was this place? A torture chamber? A fighting arena? So many things crossed her mind. She was distracted, her thoughts elsewhere when she felt a searing hot pain in her left shoulder. It caused her to drop to one knee, the pain excruciating. She turned to find the source and immediately understood what had happened. She had been shot. Shot by a man who stood a few feet away.

Bright, blinding lights began to shine in her direction. The man continued moving closer to her, his gun aimed at all times. When he stood only inches from her, she was able to get a good look at his features. He was tall and thin with dark, short cropped hair and a perfectly trimmed beard. He had blue-grey eyes, his face sallow and expressionless. His entire demeanour intimidated her. When he spoke, his voice chilled her insides.

"We finally meet," he said in his cold, empty tone.

Samantha charged her hands with electricity, getting ready for a fight. He examined her with the utmost interest, as if appraising her.

"You know, Miss O'Connor, you are the spitting image of your father. He and I never did see eye to eye on many things. He did not agree on the way I conducted my research or with my methods and still, I found the necessary leverage to convince him of participating."

Samantha did not make a move. Her hands remained charged, yet she did not dare release an attack.

"Will you listen to me? Going on and on about the past without having properly introduced myself. Forgive me for my lack of manners. I am Oleander Snyde. It is beyond a pleasure to finally meet you."

Samantha's heart beat faster at the sound of his name. There was no more running, he had her just where he wanted her. She did not say a word, the pain in her shoulder was subsiding but there was something odd, she felt dizzy, weak. The electricity she had charged before was losing strength and flickered in her hands until it was extinguished. Snyde turned his mouth into a sinister smile.

CHAPTER TWENTY EIGHT

"Miss O'Connor, I must admit, you have been a terrible burden for me," Snyde said, his tone cold and calm. He still gripped the gun tightly in his right hand.

"So sorry about that," Samantha finally spoke.

She felt exhausted. What was happening to her? It was taking most of her strength just to stay on her feet.

"Forgive me, but you don't look too well. If you are feeling *odd* let me assure you, the effects are only temporary... But, it should give me plenty of time to get what I want."

"What do you mean?" She shook her head trying to clear it. Her vision was blurred.

"Allow me to explain. This is no ordinary weapon, nor are the bullets it fires. They are coated with a new test serum, created for the sole purpose of not only causing as much harm to your body as possible but, also binding your powers temporarily. Your friend Mr. Clarke was very helpful in its creation and testing."

She felt her stomach tighten at the mention on Michael's name.

"Where is he? What have you done with him?!"

"He is of no further importance. He served his purpose and, I must admit, I have no idea where he could possibly be now."

Samantha threw herself towards Snyde with all the strength she could muster. She tried to land a punch, but he was too quick.

"Now, now, Miss O'Connor. Save your strength. There is no need to act so uncivilized. I thought we could have an honest conversation."

"I have nothing to talk about," she growled.

"Pity… You can listen. Ever since you were a young girl I knew you would have amazing powers. You displayed such strength, such mastery of your abilities. And then, you were snatched away from this facility. From your *home*. I always hoped you would return one day. You see, I believe you and I can make an unstoppable team."

Samantha could not believe what she was hearing.

"You are insane! I would never work with anyone as vile and evil as you! I would rather die."

Once again, he smiled. "I admire your resilience. It really is quite remarkable. You have managed to escape every one of my attacks unscathed. You have defeated my men, defeated my War Dogs – and most importantly – you defeated my Behemoth. Perhaps, it has all been luck. The time for luck has run out."

He paced around Samantha, still aiming the gun at her. She didn't speak. She was scoping the room, looking for something – anything – that could help her get out of this alive.

"I know what you must be thinking, and honestly I don't think you'll be able to get out of this situation," remarked Snyde. "I will offer you a simple choice. I am prepared to spare your friends as long as you agree to stay and be a part of my *family*."

"You should know by now, you shouldn't underestimate me," said Samantha, even though deep down she thought he was right.

No matter how hard she tried, she couldn't see a way out. She was too exhausted and as long as he held that gun she would not be able to regain her powers.

"There is no way I am staying here willingly, so I suggest you go ahead and shoot me. I'm tired of this game."

"I don't want to kill you, Miss O'Connor. I believe I can find a more useful purpose for you," he said. "As I said, your powers are... *incredible*. And you have potential to be so much more. Join me, fight along side me, and I will give you all the power you could ever desire."

"I have no use for power," she said, although at this moment she could definitely use *her* powers. "I would rather die a thousand times over rather than join you. And like *I* said, I'm really not too big on power, but thanks for the offer."

She clutched at the place in her shoulder where the bullet had pierced her. It was healing, but not at the speed she had hoped.

"I didn't think you would accept my offer willingly," he said calmly. "But, I have other ways of convincing you. We'll just have to do this the hard way."

He fired his gun. The bullet struck her right hip, the pain was unlike anything she had felt. The wound burned and tore at her flesh from inside her body. Samantha fell to the ground. Snyde approached her and aimed his gun once again. She heard the shot, closed her eyes and waited for the excruciating pain to rip through her body once more. Nothing happened. The bullet had fallen to the floor as if it had hit an invisible barrier. Samantha forced a weak smile.

"What's happening?!" Snyde yelled. He fired two more shots with the same result.

"Looks like I'm not alone," she said, sighing with relief.

The door behind her burst open and Apollo ran into the room.

"Sam, come on, let's get out of here," said Apollo, helping her to her feet.

Snyde fired more shots at them, but they all collided with the invisible barrier. Apollo and Samantha ran out the door and into the hallway.

"You will never leave this facility alive!" Snyde called after them.

They ran back down the labyrinth of hallways, not sure where they were headed. Everything was the same, white corridors with no distinct markings or signs.

"That was amazing! How did you do that? How did you find me, Polo? How did you get through? The door was barred shut behind me."

"Too many questions to answer now! It was nothing that I couldn't manage with my abilities. I could feel your breathing, I knew you were in trouble."

"Your powers will never seize to amaze me… I don't understand how you do it. Thank you. I thought that was it for me," she said.

"There is no need to thank me," he said.

"Where is Amelia?" asked Samantha.

"I'm not sure," said Apollo, he stopped to catch his breath. "You're hurt."

"It's nothing," said Samantha, trying to hide the intense pain she was in. "We have to find her. She might be in trouble."

CHAPTER TWENTY NINE

Amelia kept walking straight ahead until she came across a giant metal door. As she stepped closer the door opened as if inviting her in. Against her better judgement and instincts, she kept moving forward. Once she stepped inside everything turned pitch black. She stopped, her heart beating a million times per minute. Had she just walked right into a trap? Maybe it was best to turn back, but as she thought this, she felt the door behind her slide close and lock.

She held her ground, her eyes adjusting to the darkness, but it was too intense to be able to see anything. She lit a small flame in her hand. The fire helped her make out the details around her. Taking a few deep breaths, she felt herself calm down. Her heartbeat slowed enough to let her brain think. Using her flames as light she noticed that the room was set up like a giant auditorium. There were rows upon rows of seats filling the large, circular room, all the way to the top, very much like a small football field.

Amelia made her way deeper into the circular room. From her left side a soft noise made her realized there was something in the room with her. She stopped and took a deep breath. There was someone – or something – moving in the darkness. She took another breath and stepped even closer. Through her fire, she saw a large metal chair perched in the middle. Strapped to the chair was a woman. Her body was limp against her restraints. Even though she had not seen this woman in many years, she recognized her immediately.

"Alex," she whispered, running to the woman's side.

Alexa was restrained and bound to the chair by tight chains with electronic padlocks unlike the rest she had encountered in the facility. She tried to destroy one of them using her powers, but nothing happened. Alexa's body was cold and limp, but she was still breathing. Maybe she had been drugged. Amelia gave her a gentle slap to the face, trying to get a response. Nothing. She tried her powers again, this time on the restraints the bound Alexa's feet. Nothing.

Suddenly, she heard something new. A strange, rustling noise behind her. She quickly spun around, getting to her feet and ready to fight if necessary. What she saw made her gasp instantly. Approaching her slowly was a woman.

This was no ordinary woman, though. The skin on her body glowed, as if it was made of fire. She was beautiful, in a somewhat terrible way. Her eyes were dark, black as Coles, empty and lifeless. Her hair flowed around her neck and shoulders, moving like flames flickering in a fireplace. She wore a skin tight black leather dress, which made the contrast of her glowing skin even more profound. She kept coming closer and closer, and Amelia stood frozen in her spot, not sure what the woman's intentions were. The woman stopped a few feet away.

When she spoke, her voice was shockingly cold, particularly for a person who appeared to be made entirely of fire. It chilled Amelia to her very core. Even though she was frightened, there was something about the woman that perplexed her and drew her in. Her initial instinct was to run, but her feet would not move.

"Don't be afraid, child," said the woman. "I'm not here to hurt you."

Amelia didn't say a word. She just stared at the woman, terrified and intrigued in equal amounts. There was something inside her that told her she knew this woman. That their paths had crossed a lifetime ago and they were bound together by something strong.

"Let me look at you."

The woman walked even closer, now standing only inches away. She held out her hand and gently reached for Amelia's face.

Amelia flinched at her touch. The woman's face showed signs of being offended for a split second, but it quickly returned to its cold, empty expression.

"Do you know who I am?"

Amelia did not answer immediately. Something deep inside her knew. This woman was the one person she had hoped to find here tonight.

"I – I have a feeling," she said, her voice breaking.

The woman smiled. "I am Kathryn Tupper," said the woman. "Your mother."

Amelia was silent, unsure what to say. After a few moments, she began to walk closer to her mother.

"I've waited so long to finally meet you," said Kathryn, in her icy cold voice. "I have dreamed of this day, when we would be together once more."

Amelia still didn't answer. What had Snyde done to her? All the experiments, they had physically transformed her mother into something more than superhuman. Amelia just stared at her, confused about what she should feel. This was her mother, yet she felt nothing but coldness emanating from this person.

"Come closer, child. I want to see how wonderful you have turned out," said Kathryn.

She stepped closer. Kathryn looked at her. For a brief moment Amelia thought she saw something in her eyes. Was it joy at reuniting with her daughter? Kathryn came closer and embraced her. Amelia felt tears slide down her cheeks. She did not remember her mother; this moment was the first real memory.

Kathryn released her and stroked her face with her hands. The flames that covered her body did not hurt Amelia. Her own resistance to fire was a protection from this.

"What did they do to you?" Amelia asked her mother, wiping away the tears that had formed in her eyes.

"That does not matter," said Kathryn. "What matters is that we are together once again. So many lost years to catch up on. There is so much about you that I wish to know, my darling daughter."

Amelia smiled. "I know, there are so many things I want to ask you, so many things to know. But, we don't have time now, we have to escape this place! I need you to help me. Help me free my friend."

Amelia pointed towards Alexa, who still sat unconscious, strapped to the ghastly chair in the middle of the room. Kathryn looked from Alexa to Amelia, not saying a word. She seemed to consider what she was about to say.

"I'm afraid... I can not help you," she said, dryly.

"What – what do you mean? We can get out of here," said Amelia. "Don't be afraid. We can help you. We can escape this place together. My friends, they're here as well. We just need to be quick."

Kathryn walked closer to Alexa, placing her hands on the back of the chair. Amelia could sense that something about this situation was not precisely right.

"This woman," said Kathryn. "You call her friend, yet, she is the one who took you from me, along with that idiot Finley. Those *fools*."

Amelia looked at her mother as she circled Alexa.

"They thought they could keep us apart forever, but they were wrong. I knew that one day we would be together again, as it was meant to be."

"Please, everything they did was to protect us," said Amelia. "Who knows what would have happened to us if we had stayed in this place."

"You would have grown up with your mother," said Kathryn, her voice filled with hatred. "You were meant to be with me. To be more powerful than any of the others. They prevented that from happening. But, no matter. After years and years of searching, I finally caught up to Finley. I had dreamed of the day when we would come face to face again, and I could repay him for what he had done."

"What do you mean?" asked Amelia, afraid of what the answer would be.

Kathryn smiled. "He was braver than I gave him credit for. He knew what would happen to him and yet, he did not reveal your location. He was determined to keep us apart. So, I had him on his knees and watched as he took his last breath."

"You… You killed Finn?"

"He deserved it. He took you from me, kept you from knowing me! We were supposed to be together! I am your mother."

"You're the woman… The one in my dreams," said Amelia. "On the rooftop."

Amelia shook her head as she slowly backed away from her mother.

"You are not my mother. You are nothing more than a monster!" screamed Amelia.

"A monster, am I? Is that what you believe? Don't be so naive. You and your ridiculous friends, thinking you are heroes. You are just children! You know nothing of life and of true power. You have no idea! The power I have the same power within you. I can teach you if you join me. Do you have any idea of all we could accomplish? Together, we can be more powerful than any other being on earth – stronger than any weapon or government in the world. People will bow to us, will serve us! I have spoken to Oleander, he agrees that you must be on our side!"

"Sorry to disappoint you, *mother*," said Amelia, her tone challenging, her hands beginning to burn. "I would much rather die here tonight than to ever, ever become like you. I will not be consumed by power. I *refuse* to be like you."

Kathryn seemed to be losing her composure. This must now have been the reunion she had expected. Then, her lips curled into a twisted, deformed grin.

"As you wish..."

Flames burst out of nowhere and surrounded Amelia and Alexa. Amelia looked back at Kathryn and shot flames of her own towards her mother. Kathryn absorbed them and let out a maniacal laugh.

"Is that all you've got? I expected so much more from you. How very *disappointing*."

Amelia sent more flames her way, stronger this time. She was draining her energy too quickly and needed to focus. Once again, Kathryn simply absorbed the fire. She began to walk towards Amelia and Alexa, who was still bound to her chains.

Amelia was determined to not show fear, no matter what happened. She would not back down. She quickly turned to Alexa and tried to burn the restraints away. It was no use. She faced Kathryn once again, who kept walking slowly towards them. The fire was getting hotter and spreading to almost every side of the room. Amelia balled her hands into fists and flames began to form around her. She aimed the flames at her mother. Her attack was stronger this time and Kathryn flinched, though quickly recovered from the attack. There was a look of shock on her face, but only for a brief moment, unsure of what had happened.

"That's more like it!" she grinned at Amelia as she spoke. "You have to really *feel* the power, feed it with your hate. You see, we are not all that different! I know what you are feeling, all the rage inside your body!"

Amelia felt anger coursing through her veins, all the way to her finger tips. More flames burst from her hands, stronger this time. She aimed at Kathryn, who in turn was ready for the attack, she absorbed the fire and release it directly towards her daughter. Amelia received the full impact and was thrown back hard, falling to the floor.

Amelia was exhausted. Her abilities could not match her mother's. This was it, her final moments. She held back tears that threatened to fall from her eyes. If she was going to die, she would die fighting, hoping to cause some damage to Kathryn, so the others could finish her off. She tried to get up but was knocked back again. Kathryn stood inches from her. She reached down and lifted Amelia up by her neck, pinning her against the wall.

"I give you a chance to have a family! To have more power that you could ever imagine! But you refuse me and now you will pay the price!"

She tightened her grip on Amelia's neck. Amelia could feel herself fading, she tried to create flames, to fight back, but it was useless. She was going to die at the hands of her own mother. There was no hope. Suddenly Kathryn let out a harsh scream and released her. Amelia fell to the ground, coughing and gasping for air, unsure of what had just happened. She looked around, trying with all her might to remain conscious.

Kathryn scrambled around, turning to face someone. There stood Apollo, face determined, and hands stretched out towards Kathryn. He was creating a force field around her, preventing her from attacking. A few feet from him was Samantha, kneeling next to Alexa's chair, trying to release her binds. Amelia tried to stay focused, but she was too weak, she fainted and lay motionless on the floor.

****

Kathryn looked furious. Murderous. She released a savage attack on the force field that restrained her. With every attack she launched, Apollo recoiled in pain.

"Hurry up, Sam!" he called out. "I can't hold her much longer!"

"You have no idea what you're doing!" Kathryn yelled out furiously. She attacked the forcefield repeatedly. "You can't possibly hold me!"

Samantha glanced over, first at Apollo then at Amelia, who still lay collapsed on the ground. Flames still surrounded them, they had to hurry and get out of here.

"I can't release her! There are digital locks on these restraints, my powers are not working," said Samantha. "Polo, you're the only one who might be able to hack through these locks."

"Well, I'm just a bit preoccupied at the moment!" Apollo called back.

"Let her go," said Samantha.

"What? Are you crazy?!"

"I can hold her back and you free Alex," said Samantha. "It's the only way."

"No, it's mental! Your powers aren't fully recovered yet. I won't let you," Apollo argued.

"We don't have time for this, Polo. I need you to trust me. My abilities are strong enough. Release her and step back, I can handle her."

Kathryn began to laugh maniacally, clearly delighted to hear this conversation.

"Do you honestly think you can defeat me, Samantha? You're just as ridiculous as your father. No matter. I killed him and now, I get the chance to do the same to you."

Samantha was momentarily distracted by her words. "You killed my father?" A feral fury like she had never felt started building up inside her, coursing through her veins, boiling her blood, clouding her thoughts.

"Hahaha!" Kathryn's laugh was crazed. "That's right! He was weak! It was so easy to finish him. Maybe you can put up a better fight."

Samantha charged her hands with electricity. This was taking all her effort, but she would not back down.

"You're not as strong as you think," said Samantha. "Time to see what you're really made of."

Kathryn stopped attacking the forcefield and took a few steps back.

Samantha stood next to Apollo and put a hand on his arm.

"Trust me, I need you to get Alex free. I can do this."

He looked sceptical, she was determined. Apollo let out a deep breath and released the forcefield. As soon as the barrier was down, Kathryn launched her attack. Samantha avoided it and released an attack of her own. Apollo ran towards Alexa and started working on her restraints.

Samantha charged her electricity as much as she could and released it. Her attack hit Kathryn directly and she was pushed back. No longer laughing, she recoiled and clutched a hand to her chest. Some of the confidence in her face had disappeared. She sent more flames towards Samantha, who tried to deflect them but was unable and fell to the ground.

Apollo looked up while still trying to release Alexa and saw Samantha fall.

"Sam!"

He ran towards her. Kathryn threw more flames their way. He stopped the flames from impacting, creating a temporary barrier around them. Samantha got to her feet.

"Go back to Alex! We have to hurry and get out of here."

Kathryn stopped her attacks and took a moment to taunt them.

"You are all pathetic! Your weakness is amusing. Three of you couldn't do any harm to me. I am going to kill each one of you. I'll enjoy burning the life out of your pathetic bodies. This is where you will die and there is nothing you can do!"

Kathryn's behaviour was arrogant. Samantha gazed past her and saw Amelia, she was stirring back to consciousness. She stood up shakily and her eyes met Samantha's. Slowly, she nodded her head. Samantha understood. They would attack together. Kathryn was letting her guard down, she was not paying attention to Amelia. Taking advantage of this moment Samantha nodded back.

They both charged their energy and released it directly at Kathryn. Samantha's attack hit Kathryn in the chest while Amelia's hit her in the back. Kathryn's eyes widened with shock for a split second and then she collapsed to the floor. She lay still in a heap on the ground. Samantha quickly ran towards Amelia. When she reached her, Amelia collapsed into her arms, sobbing into her shoulder.

"You're okay. Everything will be fine," said Samantha, putting her hands around her Amelia's face. Amelia was dazed, in shock. "Amelia, look at me. You'll be okay, yes? It's going to be alright."

Amelia nodded and wiped away her tears.

"Is she… dead?" she asked between sobs.

Samantha walked towards Kathryn. She was still alive, just unconscious.

"She's alive. We need to get out of here. Polo, you have to set Alex free now!"

"I've almost got it," he said. "Just one more restraint." As he said it, the last of her restraints burst open. Alexa seemed very dazed. "I think she's been heavily sedated."

"We'll have to carry her," said Samantha. "Are you alright to walk?" she asked Amelia, who in turn nodded.

"You're hurt," said Amelia, pointing to the large blood stain soaking Samantha's shirt where the bullets had struck her before.

"I'm fine," she brushed it off. "It's nothing that won't heal."

"We've got to get out of here," said Apollo. "We need to find Michael… and I mean quickly. I don't know how much longer we can fight them off."

"Okay, let's keep going. There is no point being careful now. Let's just move as fast as we can."

Samantha helped Amelia to her feet and put her arm over her shoulder for support.

"We have to keep going forward, there's nothing back where we came from," Apollo pointed out.

There was another door on the opposite side of the room from where they had entered. This was the way they had to go. The group moved forward, hoping that their ordeal would soon be over.

CHAPTER THIRTY

This new door led them down yet another corridor, this one however, was a bit different from the ones they had seen before. It was a large prison block, with metal cages lining the walls. Apollo was still carrying Alexa, though she seemed to be regaining consciousness as they moved. She mumbled words under her breath every now and then.

Amelia quickly recovered her strength and walked on her own. They proceeded cautiously. Apollo stopped to inspect one of the cage-like enclosures. The outside walls were made of a rusted metal, and in the centre, there was glass, like a porthole, so you could see inside. The first cage he inspected was empty, but there were chains dangling from the walls and ceiling, as if to hang and bind prisoners.

They continued to inspect each one of the metal cages, each time peering through the glass to check if anyone was being held inside. There was an eerie sensation emanating from this place.

Apollo gently set Alexa down and stopped to inspect one particular cage where dry blood lined the outside walls. This sent a chill down his spine, thinking about the people that must have been kept here. These were torture chambers, her was certain of it. He knew that Snyde was not afraid to torture, he had seen that from the photos in Michael's file. Just the thought of it made him feel sick again. He still had the file in his pack, but he hadn't had a chance to show Samantha… or maybe he just didn't want to show her. She would feel such guilt and pain once she saw what had been done to him. He wanted to spare her those feelings for as long as he could – forever, if possible.

Apollo was deep in thought when he heard his name called out frantically.

"Polo! Over here, quick!" Amelia called out.

He ran over to where they stood, a few feet down the row of cells. Samantha was transfixed, staring into the glass. When he reached her side he immediately saw what she was staring at. This particular enclosure wasn't empty. In the middle of the room was Michael. His body held up only by the heavy chains that bound his arms to the ceiling.

"We have to get him out of there," whispered Amelia.

"There are no locks on these doors," Apollo noted. He looked back at Samantha, who still hadn't said a word. She simply stared at the broken figure, chained and trapped like he was disposable, as though his life was worth nothing.

"There has to be *some* way to open it!"

They were all silent for a few seconds, then Samantha spoke. Her voice sounded dry and distant, as if there was no emotion left in her. It was hard to know what was going through her mind at that very moment.

"Use your powers, Polo."

She turned to face him, her eyes showed so much pain that it hurt him to see her this way.

"Use your powers to bend the air around the door. You can bend the air pockets around the metal, the door should latch out of place."

"Sam, I don't know if I can do that," he whispered.

"Will you just try it?" her voice was a bit harsh, but he wasn't going to argue with her at this moment.

He turned to face the door and focused as hard as he could on the air between the cage's door. Nothing happened. He looked back at the others, both girls had their eyes fixed on the cage.

Once again, he concentrated as hard as he could. Sweat began to drip down his forehead. This time, the door began to squeak. There was a sound of metal against metal as the door wiggled and writhed on its hinges, until suddenly, it burst open.

Samantha ran inside. She knelt beside Michael and ran her hands through his hair, across his face, desperately checking for signs of life.

"Mikey, please talk to me. Please, be okay!"

Michael stirred at her touch. He lifted his face to meet hers. It took what little strength and energy he had left. His body showed recent signs of damage. His face, chest and arms were badly bruised, and some gashes were still visible around his neck.

"Sammy?" he whispered, his voice coarse and damaged, as if it had not been used for days.

Samantha breathed a huge sigh of relief and made a sound that was halfway between a laugh and a cry. Tears streamed down her cheeks and she wiped them away.

"Yes, it's me," she gently touched his face. "What have they done to you?"

She looked at the state he was in, his hair long and unkept, a thick beard covered his once clean-shaven face, scars painted his arms and back. The severity of his injuries must have been unthinkable and constant to leave scarring like this. Because of their healing abilities, none of them had ever scarred.

"We're going to get you out of here. Polo, can you break his chains?"

He nodded and concentrated, as he had done before, on the air between the thick cuffs around his wrists and began to expand them. They burst open after a few seconds, releasing Michael from his restraints. He collapsed forward into Samantha's arms.

Michael looked at her as though he was unsure if she was really there. He touched her face, her hair, her lips.

"You're really here," he whispered.

"Of course I am," said Samantha, tears continued to fall down her face. "We all are. We came for you."

Michael wiped the tears from her cheeks, pulled her closer and kissed her. Apollo turned away from them and went to stand beside Amelia, who watched on in silence. If ever there was an awkward moment, this was it. Samantha pulled away slowly from Michael's kiss. He turned to the others, as if noticing them for the first time.

"You guys shouldn't have come for me. It's crazy! This is what Snyde wanted! He wanted us all together. You have no idea how dangerous this place is."

"We're starting to get the idea," said Amelia. "I'm Amelia, by the way."

"We'll have time to catch up later," said Samantha, wiping the rest of her tears away, getting up and helping Michael to his feet. "We have to get out of here."

Samantha looked at Apollo, but he looked away. He was fighting with an urge to punch Michael, even though none of this was his fault. Hopefully they would have time to fix things later, now they had to focus on leaving this place behind.

"Polo, is there any chance you can help me get this off?" Michael pulled up his pant leg, revealing a thick black cuff around his ankle.

"What is that?"

"It's to prevent me from using my powers. I've had it on since I was captured, so I wouldn't be able to defend myself against them."

"Does it work on all of us?" Amelia asked, coming in closer to inspect the cuff.

"I think so."

"Then, why do you think they haven't tried to put these on us today? It would make capturing us much easier," Apollo added.

"It's not that simple," said Michael. "When they took me, they used large doses of a heavy sedative, to keep me knocked out. Then, they drew samples of my blood and combined it with one of their serums. They injected that into this cuff and attached it to me. The cuff is attached by three small needles that feed the serum into my system and prevent me from using my powers."

"Snyde has a weapon that has that same effect," said Samantha. "But, the effects are temporary. He used it on me tonight."

Apollo and Amelia looked at her silently. Michael nodded.

"Yes, he keeps on perfecting his serums," said Michael. "He tests them on me to know how effective they will be in combat."

"Combat?" Apollo asked. "This isn't a war."

"It is to him," said Michael. "What he's planning, it's so much more than just capturing us."

"This a lot to take in!" Amelia squeaked.

Michael simply nodded.

"I can try removing it by force, but it may hurt," said Apollo, refocusing on the cuff.

"That doesn't matter," Michael answered in a hollow tone. "Pain doesn't feel the same for me anymore."

Apollo used his powers to pry the cuff from Michael's body. Blood dripped from his leg, but his face showed no signs of discomfort from the wound.

"Thanks."

"How do you feel? Can you use your powers now?" asked Samantha.

Michael held out his hand and a small water orb began to form around it. He used the water to wash the blood dripping down his leg.

"I felt weak and dizzy just from that small effort, but I should be okay. I don't know how useful I'll be in a fight."

"Let's hope it doesn't come to that," said Apollo. "We have to go, let's find the fastest way out of here." He turned around to leave, the others followed.

"Wait," said Michael, as the others stepped out of the cage. "Alex... she's here…"

"Don't worry, she's alright, she's with us."

No sooner had Amelia spoken these words than there was a terrible scream. They ran outside to find three enormous War Dogs surrounding Alexa.

"These guys again? I mean, seriously, I've had enough of this," said Samantha.

One of the War Dogs turned its attention to them, launching itself forward, jaw wide open, ready to attack. Apollo tried to create a barrier to stop it attacking, but he was too slow and the creature bit deep into his leg, dragging him away from the others.

****

Amelia shot out fierce flames in an attempt to have the dog release Apollo, but the dog didn't even flinch, it held its victim tightly in its jaw. As she prepared to fire again Michael stopped her.

"What are you doing?" Amelia asked.

"Don't use your powers on them!" he exclaimed.

"Are you crazy?"

"They'll just absorb our powers and use them against us. Trust me!"

231

"Would you like to venture any suggestions, Mikey?" asked Samantha, she charged her hands with electricity.

"Just follow my lead," said Michael, determination etched on his face.

Michael needed what was left of his energy for this. He ran full speed towards the War Dog that had Apollo. The dog turned its attention to Michael as he approached but it was too slow, and Michael managed to jump over it and latch onto its back.

The dog growled in annoyance and released Apollo, turning its attention to Michael instead. Samantha went to Apollo's side, his leg bleeding badly, a deep gash could be seen through his ripped jeans.

"I'm okay, it'll heal quickly," he said, gritting his teeth.

Michael continued to grasp onto the large beast's back, the creature snapping its jaw back and forth, trying to knock him off, to no avail. Once he was certain that the dog was only focusing on him, Michael jumped off and ran towards one of the empty cages surrounding the room. The dog chased after him, his body transforming into what looked like hot embers. It was furious and in close pursuit.

"Mikey, what are you doing?" Samantha called after him.

"It's okay, I've got a plan! Trust me," he called back. He entered the empty cage and the dog followed. "Polo, lock me in the cage!"

"Are you crazy? That thing will rip to to shreds!"

"Do it, now!"

Apollo did as he was told, locking the door to the cage, leaving Michael trapped inside with the raging War Dog.

Samantha ran towards the cage and peered through the glass. In the middle of the small cell stood Michael, but the cage was now completely filled with water. He was able to breathe underwater no problem, the War Dog however, was not. The creature writhed back and forth in the water, trying to find a way out, to no avail. After a couple of minutes struggling, unable to find a source of oxygen, it stopped moving.

Michael drained the room of water and fell to his knees.

"Open the door, Polo," Samantha commanded.

Apollo released his grip on the door. Samantha ran inside to help Michael.

"You shouldn't have done that; your powers are still recovering."

"It was nothing," said Michael, slightly out of breath. "You know it will take more than that to take me down." He touched her face. "I still can't believe you're actually here."

Samantha was silent.

"Come on," she cleared her throat. "There's still two more to go."

When they stepped out, there was Apollo, still laying on the floor, with Amelia at his side. A few feet away the other two War Dogs still had their attention on Alexa, who appeared to have fainted again.

Suddenly, one of the dogs seemed to noticed them and strayed away from their target. He began to come closer to where Apollo and Amelia were. Samantha charged her hands and ran towards the creature. Michael tried to stop her but was too slow for her.

"Sammy, don't!"

Too late, she had reached the dog and had jumped onto its back, like Michael had done minutes before. The dog growled with anger and tried to get her off, she held tightly, electricity coursing from her hands straight into the dog's body. It let out a howl of pain, which sent out a signal to the remaining dog. The last War Dogs grabbed Alexa and dragged her as fast as it could away from the room. It disappeared, taking her with it before any of them could react.

****

Samantha continued to latch onto the dog, until she felt it begin to weaken. The dog no longer howled in anger but yelped with pain. The direct contact with the electricity was too much for it to handle, it was burning its insides, organs failing, slowly ending its life.

Once she was certain the creature was dead, Samantha let go. The amount of energy she generated was too much, she was weak, though she was trying very hard to not show it. She grasped her shoulder, where the bullet had entered earlier. The wound had reopened, fresh blood seeping from it again.

"Are you okay, Sam?" Amelia asked.

"I'm fine," she answered, avoiding any direct eye contact.

Amelia did not look convinced, but she didn't press the matter further. Michael walked over to Apollo and helped him up.

"We have to go back for Alex," said Apollo.

"No," said Michael. The others all stared at him.

"A minute ago, you said we had to get her, now you want to just leave her behind?" said Amelia. "We can't do that! Who knows what they'll do to her."

"I know what I said, but we're not strong enough. It's not my intention to sound so harsh, but she would want us to leave her and save ourselves. She told me so, countless times. She told me that if I ever found a way out to not even think about losing the opportunity by trying to go after her."

"She has been through hell and back for us," said Apollo, his voice rising with anger. "She gave up her entire life to save us! And you want to just leave her here? To be tortured and tested and God knows what else."

"Why don't you grow up, Polo? Look around, Sam's hurt, you can barely stand straight," Michael said. "And, no offense but you look like you've been to hell and back." He pointed to Amelia.

"Alex made her choices, no one forced her to save us or to even get involved with this place at all. She and Finn knew full well what they were getting into. They knew much better than they ever told us. The only reason they ever decided to get us out, was so they could live with the guilt of what they had done," said Michael.

"What do you mean?" asked Amelia.

"There is so much more to this than we ever knew," said Michael. "We had no idea how big Snyde's plans were."

"But you know now?" asked Samantha.

"I've learned a lot from my time here," he said, his voice softer with her than with the others. "I will tell you everything I know, but right now we need to focus on getting out."

The others still weren't convinced about leaving Alexa behind. Michael took a deep breath, clearly annoyed at their insistence.

"Listen, they won't hurt her. They need her, she wasn't tortured like I was. They need her for what she knows… it's a long story, I can't tell now. But, I need you to believe me. We will get her back, but we need to be better prepared. We can't save her on our own."

Samantha looked at him, analysing the situation. He was right, they were all hurt, tired, powered out. They needed to get out of this place as soon as possible or they risked never leaving at all. She nodded her head at Michael.

"Fine, Mikey. Help us get out of here. You've been here for a long time; can you show us the best way?"

He nodded. "We have to keep going this way." He pointed to the door on the other end of the room. "The security control room is a few doors down. From there we can hack into the security system and clear a path for us to escape."

"Then that's what we'll do." Samantha looked over at Apollo.

For the first time in their lives she couldn't read him. She wanted so badly to reach out to him, have him hold her, comfort her. She needed to talk to him in private, to explain everything she was feeling, but that would have to wait for later – if they had a later.

CHAPTER THIRTY ONE

They made their way carefully down a few more doors, finding nothing in their way. Finally, they arrived at the central security control room. The room itself was incredible, computer screens filled every inch of it, with a main computer enclosed in a glass dome in the middle of the room and several smaller screens and keypads surrounding the rest.

Amelia felt exhaustion taking over. It was clear that this last battle with the newly enhanced War Dogs had left the four of them drained. Michael had clearly still not recovered his strength from all the time he had been forced to wear the cuff around his ankle. Apollo was shaking, Michael helping him stand because of his injured leg. Samantha tried to appear calm and in control as she always did, but her wounds were not healing correctly, blood still dripped from her shoulder and hip.

Amelia was afraid, after all they had been through tonight, she had never been more unsure about what would happen next. They had no real plan, no easy escape route. She felt trapped.

As if things weren't already bad enough, an alarm started wailing, red lights flashed around them. It was clear that Snyde was not going to take any more chances, he knew they had gotten further than he would have hoped. Amelia was certain that now every single guard and soldier he had at his disposal would be coming for them.

"We've got to find a way out of here... Fast," said Samantha, pacing the room, looking at the many screens in front of them.

As they watched the security screens, their eyes grew wide with horror. Each monitor began to show the glossy white corridors filling with armoured soldiers and what was left of the enhanced animals.

Amelia couldn't stop thinking that it was near impossible to find a way out. They were outnumbered, and their powers needed rest. They were too tired to be able to fight their way out from all this. They would be captured and this time, she wasn't convinced that they would be shown any mercy.

"Polo, this is the main security terminal," said Michael, pointing to the enclosed computer in the centre of the room. "You think you can hack your way in? Disable the security systems and unlock all the doors."

"Would that give us a chance to escape?" asked Amelia.

"I don't know..." Apollo stuttered. "I've never tried to hack into something this complex."

"This seems like the time to try," said Samantha, determination in her voice. "Mikey, you've been in this facility for almost a year. Once Polo disables the systems, are you able to navigate us through the halls and tunnels to find the fastest way out?"

"I think so," said Michael. "I've only been in this room once before, but I'm pretty sure I can find the way."

He smiled at her. Amelia felt her heart sink a little. She thought about how Samantha had fought so hard to find Michael, it would tear her heart to think that something could happen to either of them. Amelia fought back tears that were building in her eyes. There would be time to shed them later, now was a time to stay focused on the problem at hand.

Shots were heard from a distance. They glanced at the screens and saw the guards closing in on them. Soon they would be here.

"Okay, Polo, get started," said Samantha. "Create as strong a force field around yourself as you can. We'll hold them off while you try to deactivate the security systems."

Apollo nodded and began to work. Creating a force field around himself and the central computer. He had to focus as much energy as he could to make sure nothing could penetrate it.

Shots were fired at the door.

"Let's get this party started, shall we?" said Michael, a wide grin on his face.

The three of them took cover. Michael and Amelia behind a large pillar in the middle of the large room and Samantha behind a row of desks. The door exploded, scattering debris all around. At least two dozen guards stormed into the room. As soon as the guards stepped in, the trio stepped out of cover and fired their attacks.

Samantha released bolts of electricity that hit a couple of guards directly on their chests. They collapsed. Amelia fired a stream of flames at another group of guards, but they avoided the fire and took cover of their own. They fired round after round, trying to hit anything they could. One bullet hit Samantha's side. She moaned in pain and crouched further into her cover.

Apollo turned to see what was going on. He saw Samantha clutching at her side in pain, blood drenching her shirt. "Sam!" He called out.

"Don't worry about me, Polo! Please, just keep going," she called back. "You're our best chance of getting out of here."

Michael turned furiously on the guards. Two giant whirlpools were forming around either side of them. They looked shocked, unsure of what to do next. The whirlpools closed in around them, trapping the guards inside. They dropped their weapons and gasped for air. They were drowning, struggling as the water filled their lungs.

Michael looked beside himself, a bit deranged. Anger taking over every inch of his being. Amelia sensed his anger. She understood all he had felt, all the hatred he had inside, all the months of torture. He was taking it all out on these guards.

"Michael, stop!" Amelia called to him. She stood next to him, taking hold of his arm. "We're not like them! We're not killers!"

"After all they've done to us and all the pain they've caused, you want to show them mercy?" He sneered.

"I won't let them take our humanity as well. I won't become like them."

Michael stared at Amelia and seemed to calm down. He then looked back at Samantha, who was back on her feet.

"Listen to her, Mikey," she said. "Let's just get out of here."

Michael released the whirlpools and the guards dropped unconscious to the floor.

"How's it going, Polo?" Michael called out.

"You want the good news first?" Apollo called back.

"Not if there's bad news after!"

"How about the bad news first then?!"

"Just tell us already, Polo!" Samantha demanded.

"I've managed to hack through a first layer of the security system, which is allowing me to deactivate most of the doors and gates," said Apollo.

"That's not so bad, is it?" asked Amelia.

"That was the good news, now the bad one. I'll have to deactivate each door one by one and that'll take too much time, in case you haven't noticed, time isn't a luxury we have at the moment."

"There's more bad news," said Michael, pointing to the monitors to their right.

Dozens and dozens of new guards were coming their way again, there seemed to be an endless supply of reinforcements heading for them.

"Great, so I guess we'll just die, how does that sound?" said Apollo.

"I would really rather not," squeaked Amelia. "There has to be something we can do. We've come too far for it to end like this."

No one said anything.

"Let's not all talk at once, please! Too many ideas can be overwhelming!" said Apollo.

"Will you stop with the jokes, Polo, before I kick your ass," said Michael.

They both started arguing. "Both of you, shut up!" yelled Samantha. Then she turned to Apollo. "There is one other option. Polo, do you remember what you promised me?"

"Sam, don't even think about it," he said, getting up from his chair and walking up to her.

"What promise? What are you talking about?" Michael asked, looking from one to the other. Neither of them seemed to listen.

"I knew it might come to this and I need to know that you'll do what you promised," said Samantha, a mixture of determination and defiance filled her voice.

"I'm really confused now," added Amelia, she looked at Michael, who appeared to be just as baffled.

"Sam, I can't. Please, don't make me do this," said Apollo. "I'm not strong enough."

Whatever was going on between Apollo and Samantha was clearly not going to be explained and Amelia felt like she had stepped into a private moment she would gladly have walked away from if given the choice.

****

Samantha stepped closer to Apollo and grabbed his face with both her hands.

"I need you to be strong enough," she whispered. "I'm so sorry, I hope you can forgive me for this someday." She fought back tears that were building in her eyes. "You deserve better than me, Polo."

She backed away from him. "Sammy, what's going on?" Michael asked gently.

Michael took Samantha's hand and turned her towards him. He looked worried – scared. She had never seen him this way, but her decision was already made.

"I didn't want things to be this way," she said to Michael. "Promise me you will take care of them, no matter what happens."

She leaned forward and kissed him softly.

"What? –" Michael began to say. Samantha backed away from him.

Footsteps could be heard in the distance. The guards were coming again. This time more than they could handle.

"When I tell you, put up a forcefield around yourself and the others, Polo," said Samantha. "There's no more time."

"Please. Don't," Apollo begged.

"Now!" She yelled at him.

Before anyone could say or do anything else, Apollo surrounded Michael, Amelia and himself in a forcefield. Michael slammed his fists against the newly formed transparent wall.

"What the hell are you doing?!" he demanded. "Let down the forcefield, Polo! Do it, now!"

Samantha turned her back to them and closed her eyes in deep concentration. Sparks shot out from all the computers and lights around the room.

Both Amelia and Michael understood what Samantha was doing. She was going to shut down the whole base with her abilities, absorbing all the electricity that powered it, taking on much more energy than her body could possibly hold, sacrificing herself in the process.

"Sam, don't do this! We'll find another way," she yelled, tears trickling down her cheeks.

Lights flickered madly on and off all around them. They could hear distant explosions, the ground felt like it was quaking. The building could not handle this much damage, the structure wouldn't hold on for much longer. The entire facility would collapse around them.

Samantha fell to her knees and let out an earsplitting scream, yet she did not stop. She was absorbing too much energy and it was destroying body. She felt electricity course through her veins like never before, ripping through her body. It was causing her excruciating pain. Te others could do nothing except watch in horror. At that instant, more guards entered the room.

Samantha turned her attention to them. Now she was not only absorbing the electricity around her, she was also focusing her powers on generating enough energy to knock out all the guards.

"Sam, NOOOOOOOO!" Amelia yelled. Tears flowing freely down her face. "We can help you! You don't have to do this all on your own."

One by one, the guards collapsed, as more and more explosions were heard from afar. Everything around them shook violently.

****

After what felt like an eternity, the lights stopped flickering and they were left in total darkness.

"Ames, we need some light." Apollo was the first to break the eerie silence.

Amelia created a small flame in her left hand. With this light they could see the destruction around them. The computers had exploded, chunks of debris scattered from the walls caused by the explosions around the compound. Thick dust filled the room. In front of them, they saw Samantha, lifeless on the floor.

"Release the forcefield now, Polo," said Amelia.

He was numb, in shock, but he did as he was told. Michael ran to Samantha's side. She wasn't breathing. He checked for her pulse but there was none. She was gone. Tears ran down Michael's face. He let out a terrible scream. Amelia knelt beside him and put her arm around his shoulder.

"We have to go," she said to him.

"No! I'm not going to leave her here." He wiped the tears away from his eyes. "Polo, help me carry her! Come on! Why won't you help me?"

At that moment there was another explosion just outside. "We have to go," said Amelia, gently. "She wanted us to be safe. We can't help her anymore. Please, Michael. She died for us. We have to go." She tried to pull him to his feet, but he refused to move. Apollo came over to them.

"Mikey, this is what she wanted. It's time to go."

CHAPTER THIRTY TWO

They ran down countless dark hallways, trying to navigate the maze filled with rubble and debris, their only light coming from Amelia's flame as she led the way.

"Turn left here," said Michael.

No one had spoken much since they left Samantha's body behind. Only the few instructions given by Michael to get them out of the lab. With each new path they found unconscious guards struck down by the electric energy Samantha had released. Their escape was easy. She had saved them, given up everything to keep them from harm.

After what seemed like hours, they reached the exit to the lab. The sun was shining bright outside, almost blinding after being in darkness for so long.

The three of them stood in silence, side by side. Each lost in their own thoughts and concerns. They made their way back to the truck in complete silence. When they reached it, Michael climbed into the driver's seat and the other two sat in the back seats.

"So, what now?" asked Amelia, her voice choking back a sob.

"We have to stop Snyde and your lunatic mother," Michael answered, his voice strong and determined.

"That *thing* is not my mother," said Amelia.

"We have to avenge Sam's death," Apollo added.

"And get Alexa back," said Amelia.

"So, save the world from two maniacs and their army of genetically modified soldiers, save Alexa, avenge Sam's death and walk out of this alive," said Michael. "Sounds easy enough."

They all managed to smile.

"One day at a time?"

"Are we going back to The Bunker?" Amelia asked.

"No," said Michael. "There's nothing for us there anymore. We have to move forward."

"Where *are* we going, then?" Amelia asked him.

"We have to get to Washington, D.C.," said Michael.

"What's in Washington?"

"There is someone there who can help us," said Michael.

"What do you mean? Who can help us?" asked Apollo, his curiosity levels spiking.

"I'll explain everything on the way, but trust me, we're not as alone as we always thought," Michael answered.

The other two exchanged looks of bewilderment. They had allies out there, people who might be able to help them be safe and stop Snyde's plans. Perhaps there was hope after all. Hope for happiness, hope for safety, hope of a future. However uncertain that future may be, there was no turning back now.

****

Oleander Snyde walked amongst what remained of his precious facility. He had worked so hard to build it. So many years he had dedicated to his life's work and now all that remained was destruction, dust and rubble. They would pay for this. For taking something that was so dear to him. So much damage done by four individuals. He would make sure that each one would suffer a fate worse than death. He guaranteed it.

He stepped into what remained of the security control room and slowly approached the figure lying still in the middle. After a few minutes Kathryn appeared beside him, escorted by a few guards.

"Check her," said Snyde.

A guard quickly knelt beside Samantha's still body.

"Well?" asked Kathryn in her cold, sinister voice.

"There's a pulse, sir," the guard answered. "It's very weak, but its there."

Snyde smiled. "Excellent. Take her to the new facility… I have big plans for her."

Twitter: @mg_coll
Instagram: M.G_Coll

www.ingramcontent.com/pod-product-compliance
Lightning Source LLC
Chambersburg PA
CBHW070554130626
46556CB00001B/151